LISA FOX

When I was young, I wanted to be a lawyer when I grew up. But then I changed my mind because being a famous, yet totally undercover secret agent would be much cooler. I looked into it, but there weren't many job opportunities. I thought for a while and concluded that maybe I should just marry well. People make whole careers of that. I fell deeply in love with Agent Mulder, but he already had Scully, and I don't share.

So, instead, I became a writer.

Now I get to be all of those things and so many more.

One Kiss

LISA FOX

Harper*Impulse* an imprint of
HarperCollins*Publishers* Ltd
77–85 Fulham Palace Road
Hammersmith, London W6 8JB

www.harpercollins.co.uk

A Paperback Original 2014

First published in Great Britain in ebook format by Harper*Impulse* 2014

Copyright © Lisa Fox 2014

Cover Images © Shutterstock.com

Lisa Fox asserts the moral right to
be identified as the author of this work

A catalogue record for this book
is available from the British Library

ISBN: 978-0-00-759190-9

This novel is entirely a work of fiction.
The names, characters and incidents portrayed in it are
the work of the author's imagination. Any resemblance to
actual persons, living or dead, events or localities is
entirely coincidental.

Automatically produced by Atomik ePublisher from Easypress

*I wholeheartedly dedicate this book to
Allison Gibbons, Sara Brookes,
and Kacey Hammell. Thank you.*

Chapter One

Kat spun around when her cell phone rang, and the stiletto heel on her brand-new shoes snapped, knocking her off-balance. She crashed down on the living-room carpet with a loud thump, grunting out a string of vile curses. Her short, sparkly dress twisted around her hips as she scrambled to get up, and a few sequins fell off when she collided with the coffee table. The phone slid off the glass top, bounced twice, and hit the floor. She snatched it off the ground as the last bars of "Tank!" played, brought it to her ear, and winced as the missed-call beep blasted her eardrum.

"Son of a bitch," she muttered, and checked the caller ID to see who had caused her all this grief. Dean. It figured. Her eyebrows furrowed. She hadn't expected to hear from him for another few days. He was supposed to be out somewhere swanky tonight, spending a very expensive, very exclusive New Year's Eve with his girlfriend, Marine. The more expensive, the better. Marine wouldn't settle for anything less. And she would not be happy if she knew he was calling Kat in the middle of their date. There had to be something wrong.

She slipped off her broken shoes as she called him back, grimacing when she tossed them into the trash can. It was a damn tragedy to have to throw out a cute pair of shoes. This was not a positive omen for the evening.

"Hey, Kat," he answered on the second ring, and the familiar sound of his deep voice made her smile. Dean had a way of always making her smile. He also had a way of getting under her skin and driving her crazy too, but right now it was good to hear his voice. She'd missed him a lot during the Christmas break.

"Hey, yourself." She switched the phone to her other ear and pushed open her bedroom door. Going out tonight was probably a bad idea. She was beginning to regret letting Ron talk her into this ridiculous blind date. If there was any time left to back out, she would have. Well, maybe that wasn't entirely true. She was kind of excited. Curious anyway. She'd been so stagnant lately. It was time to shake things up. "What's going on?"

"Nothing. I just got back and I wanted to say hi."

"Huh-huh," she said, allowing him to hear the skepticism in her voice. This was not a "just say hi" call. Something was up. She could feel it. "I thought you'd be out with Marine by now." She knelt down in front of her closet and pushed her half-unpacked suitcases aside. Her shoulders sagged as she peered into the dark, chaotic recesses. She was never going to find anything in there. Why had she never organized? Maybe that ought to be her New Year's resolution. She dug around and pulled out a pair of red, patent-leather Mary Jane's, which she examined and promptly tossed aside. Definitely not right. "What are you guys doing tonight?"

He took a deep breath and exhaled. "Mari and I broke up."

Kat sat back on her heels. That was news—and not the bad kind. The last time she'd seen them together, Marine had been clinging to Dean's arm as hard as usual. *Found someone with a bigger wallet, did she?* formed on her lips, but she bit the words back. He knew exactly how she felt about Marine. He didn't need to hear it right now. "What happened?"

She heard the phone shift and knew that he was raking his fingers through his thick, curly hair. It was what he did whenever he was upset. "It started out like it always does, you know? She bitched about my job, cried over all the money I was 'losing' by not going somewhere else, and then she got all twisted, went on this rampage about how we can't get married if—"

"Whoa, whoa, *whoa*." She shook her head so violently, her hair got caught on a button of the only business suit she owned. She winced as she pulled herself free, ripping out a fair amount of hair in the process. "Please don't tell me you proposed to her?"

"What? No. But it's what she wants."

I'll bet. Marine was no fool. She was entering her late twenties and while she was a working model, she wasn't one of the elite. One day very soon she was going to be nothing more than an old face in a sea of younger, fresher faces. For women like Marine, marrying well became the next logical step. Dean was an excellent candidate. He was young, ambitious, an award-winning designer on the ground floor of a successful boutique web design and marketing firm. He'd already been headhunted a number of times by the corporate giants. If he ever decided to make a move, he'd be able to name his price. And, as an added bonus, he looked great in a suit. "I don't understand. You broke up over that? You guys have had that fight a million times before."

"Well, this time when she left, I didn't stop her." He paused. "I haven't heard from her since."

Good riddance, she almost said aloud. He deserved so much better. "When was this?"

"Tuesday." She heard him sit down on his couch, the familiar creak of the springs in the background. "Right after the holiday dinner."

Kat's mouth dropped open. "Before Christmas? Dean, that was over a week ago! You're just telling me now?"

She could feel him shrug, see his sheepish grin. "You were in California and I only got back from Colorado last night. There was nothing you could do."

She huffed in reply and dove back into the closet. There was probably something she should be saying, some comfort she should be offering, but he didn't really sound all that upset, and a deep, mean, little part of her was glad Marine was gone. A deep, selfish little part of her actually rejoiced. "So, what happens now?"

He didn't get a chance to answer because Kat yelped as a pile of boxes fell down around her head.

"Kat," he called, his voice sharp with alarm. "Are you all right?"

She couldn't help but smile. She knew without any doubt that he was on his feet, that he'd leapt up the moment she screamed, and was ready to jet over to her place to save her immediately. Sir Galahad had nothing on Dean. Sickening as it was, it never failed to strum a cord way back in the depths of her black little heart. She wasn't used to people wanting to care for her and every time he did, it left her feeling a bit unbalanced, yet oddly touched. But, no matter how sweet, it was the reason behind most of his problems. He was a sucker for a female in distress—or at least the ones who were convincingly in distress.

"I'm fine," she said, pressing her palm against the side of her head where the corner of a box had struck. She supposed she should have been grateful there was no blood. A great, big river of blood gushing out of her head would only have made the night that much more awesome. "I'm trying to get ready for Ron and Alan's party."

"I didn't think you were going."

"I wasn't." She had intended to stay home and work, maybe have a glass of champagne alone at midnight, but then Ron approached her the day after the holiday dinner with his idea, and she had randomly said yes, surprising both him and herself. A sigh escaped her lips as her gaze touched the disarray spanning out into the center of her bedroom. She should have stuck with her original plan.

"So," he said, drawing out the word. "What changed?"

She bit her lower lip. She was going to have to tell him eventually—there was no way around that—but she thought she wouldn't have to deal with it until Monday. It wasn't that she was embarrassed or anything, it was just that whenever she thought about telling him, she got this weird sensation in her gut, as though everything below her navel wanted to tighten up into a hard knot. Even now her stomach flipped, and she had to take a deep breath before speaking. "They're…" Do it quick, get it over with. "Ron and Alan are setting me up with someone."

He was silent for a full thirty seconds before bursting into laughter. "Really?"

"Yes, really." She should've known that was going to be his reaction. She braced herself for the inevitable ribbing. He loved to tease her, and while she usually found it fun, she was not quite ready to joke around or explain this to him yet. She was having a hard enough time explaining it to herself.

"Wow, Kat." He must have heard something in her voice because he didn't press it for a change. "All right then. I guess I'll let you go. Have a good time."

"Wait," she said before he could hang up. He sounded so down. Unlike her, Dean didn't thrive on solitude. He needed companionship, interaction. He'd be miserable if he spent the night alone. "Why don't you come with me?"

"Oh, no," he said, laughter returning to his voice. "This is your deal. Besides, what I am going to do while you're off having your love connection?"

She tsked. "The entire office is going to be there along with the rest of the extended family. You're going to know everybody." She shifted through the wreckage of her closet and uncovered a pair of strappy platforms she had forgotten she owned. She held them up to the light, admiring the deep-red hue, the subtle hint of sparkle. They were perfect, way better than the shoes that had broken. A total score. She slid them on and stood up. She obviously needed to check her closet more often. There was some great stuff in there. "There'll be plenty of people for you to talk to."

There was a moment of silence before he answered. "Really, Kat, I don't think I want to."

"Aw, Dean," she said, trying to keep her tone light and playful.

She didn't want him to be alone, but more than anything, that damn, annoying, selfish part of her desperately wanted him along. He was her partner in mayhem. She needed him there. "It's New Year's Eve. Let's go drink and party and meet people and get laid. That's what we're supposed to do, right? Our lives won't be worth living for the next year if we don't."

He chuckled. "You have a point."

She smiled. This was good. "I know." She stood up and caught a glimpse of herself in the mirror, her eyes widening in horror. Her hair was sticking up at crazy angles, the intricate bun that had taken her almost an hour to create was decimated. She pulled the pins out and ran her fingers through the tangled mess. She should probably redo her hair, but all these extra preparations were making her insane. If her blind date wasn't into the "I don't own a hairbrush" style then that was his problem. "I'm calling a cab now. I'll be there in twenty minutes."

"All right," he said. "I'll be waiting."

She hung up and then called the cab. It arrived quickly, an old brown Lincoln Town Car that had probably seen more of New York than she ever would. The inside smelled of Royal Pine air freshener and the stale musk of a thousand other passengers. The driver played Spanish-language Christmas music for his own listening pleasure, tapping his thumb against the wheel to the beat. Traffic was light on Flatbush and they glided down the avenue, sailing through a string of green lights. The moon was high in the sky, and it cast a sliver glow over the city streets, illuminating the well-dressed and hardly-dressed people. Kat gazed out the window, watching the Caribbean restaurants, discount shoe stores, and bodegas slowly transform into bistros and organic specialty markets as they made their way to Park Slope.

Dean was sitting on the stoop of his building when they arrived, and she grinned when he caught her eye. The sight of him always made her smile, sent a pleasantly wicked rush of heat through her body. He was just that attractive. The quintessential All-American boy, he was six-foot-two, athletic, charming, and everything about him was golden, from his wavy mass of honey-brown hair to the flecks of gold in his hazel eyes, right down to his healthy copper skin. He was the stuff of dreams, a bronzed god among the mortals. Women loved him, fawned for his attention, and there were times when Kat could actually see the sexual fantasies playing out behind their eyes while they spoke to him. She was so glad she wasn't one of his groupies. They were nauseating.

He circled the cab to the passenger's side, his camel-colored winter coat brushing against his knees as he walked. The coat was tailored to fit his broad shoulders and judging from the conservative cut, she guessed it was Burberry or one of those other preppy designers he favored. He smiled broadly as he entered the cab, the rosy flush on his cheeks from the cold night air only adding to his sexy, boy-next-door good looks.

She kissed him hello, a peck on the cheek that was their usual greeting. The light stubble on his jaw was soft and prickly against her lips and the smell of his cologne, of him, sent warmth cascading down her spine. Dean was beautiful, sweet and smart, but he was also her closest friend, and she was absolutely not his type. Nor was he hers. She preferred her men darker in both looks and personality.

Their eyes met and a spark of electricity crackled in the air between them. For one, wild, frozen second she thought he might kiss her. And that she might let him. Her cheeks flushed and her breath caught. Eternity stretched out, and then snapped in a blink, gone like it had never been there. He dropped his gaze and took her hand, lightly caressing the inside of her wrist, strumming her thready pulse. She swallowed back the heat that wanted to settle low in her belly, and when he looked back into her eyes, she smiled, her heart filled with simple, platonic affection. Nothing more.

Dean climbed into the cab and smiled when he saw Kat. He always smiled when he saw her. She was beautiful. Most people saw some typical, vapid Southern California girl when they looked at her; she embodied it with her light-blond hair, cornflower-blue eyes, and smoking beach body, but he knew better. He had seen it the first time she flashed him that dark little smile of hers. Underneath that seemingly tame exterior beat the heart of a brilliant, though somewhat warped, rebel woman and being with her was like being on a perpetual adventure, even when they were sitting on his couch playing video games.

He leaned over and kissed her cheek, breathing in her scent, the heady combination of lilac and soap that had a way of stimulating his senses. He pulled back slightly and when their eyes met an electric current zapped his nerve endings, raising the fine hair on his arms. She made some noise, or maybe exhaled a little louder than usual, and his eyes flicked to her glossy red lips, plump and slightly parted, close enough to kiss.

For a heartbeat he considered it. All he had to do was dip his head a centimeter more and his lips would be on hers, her taste in his mouth. A part of him craved the contact, demanded it, but he pushed the temptation aside. It was nothing new. He was always kind of tempted, from the moment they met. But he was with the congressman's daughter at the time, and when that ended, there was the Knicks City Dancer, and then, not much later, Marine. He might have gone for it during one of the few occasions when they were both single, but he never quite knew if she would welcome it or not. Sometimes he thought she might, other times, not so much. He decided long ago that finding out was not worth the risk. She was already his in the best possible ways. He didn't need to gamble what they shared on one kiss.

Instead, he dropped his gaze to her lap and took her hand, running his fingertips over the tattoo around her wrist, the words, "We're All Mad Here." He was with her the night she got it done, holding her other hand while she laughed through the discomfort. Afterward, they'd gone to his rooftop, drank a bottle of Jack, and danced to "Don't Stop Believin'" until the neighbors complained about the noise. It was one of his best memories.

He laced his fingers through hers and squeezed. She smiled over at him and returned the gesture. And just like that, his entire world was better.

"So, tell me about this guy," he said, breaking the comfortable silence. Teasing her was one of his favorite activities, and he wasn't about to let this prime opportunity pass him by. It had nothing to do with the niggling worm that wanted to squirm its way into his heart.

Kat snorted. "I don't really know that much. He's Alan's sister's massage therapist's brother." She waved her hand, dismissing it all. "Something like that." A lock of hair dropped in front of her face and she swiped it back behind her ear. "According to Ron, he's 'perfect for me,' whatever that means." Her hair was messier than she usually wore it, a chaotic tumble of waves that fell around her shoulders and almost looked as if she'd had a good romp in bed. He liked it. "You know how Ron and Alan are," she went on. "Just because they're happily married, they think everyone should be too." She smiled, but it looked strained. "I don't know how they talked me into it."

"I was wondering that very same thing," he said. "Are they blackmailing you or something?" Getting set-up on blind dates was very much not Kat's style. She was a notorious commitment-phobe and over the years he had known her, she'd had flings, but not much else. Agreeing to a blind date, a match from Ron no less, was completely out of character. Ron and Alan were hopeless romantics and because they wanted everyone to find their "soul mates," they often set up the Sharpe Designs family members with suitable prospects. They were good at it too—three of their matches had turned into marriages. Kat knew what agreeing to a set up like this could mean and he was surprised that she might be considering something more long-term. He wondered what had changed. And why.

"Or something." She shook her head and shrugged. "I guess

they caught me a weak, horny moment."

Dean smiled. A very typical Kat response. He tapped her knee, her stockings silky under his fingertips. She could be a hard woman, even cold at times, but her body was always soft, her skin warm and supple. "Guys are for more than just sex, you know."

"Are they?" Her eyes widened with feigned innocence. "I can't image what else I would do with one."

"Oh, I don't know, we can be handy to have around. We can lift heavy things, get the tops off most jarred products, kill spiders." He was rapidly running out of examples, and he tried to think of things his dad did that made his mother happy, grasping onto the first thing that came to mind. "Yard work."

"Yard work?" Her laugher made his insides hum. She had such a great laugh, bold and vibrant. "I live in an apartment in Brooklyn. Why would I ever need anyone to do yard work?"

He couldn't think of a single reason. "You never know," he said as enigmatically as possible.

The cab slowed down as the traffic ahead came to a grinding halt in the middle of the Manhattan Bridge. Horns honked and tires screeched, but no one was moving. He could see the Brooklyn Bridge over Kat's shoulder and the skyline was a dazzling array of sparkling lights on the horizon. The view never failed to take his breath away. He loved New York.

"How was your Christmas?" he asked. The last time they had seen one another was the night of the holiday dinner. The night he broke up with Marine.

She grimaced. "The same as it always is. My first night there, my sister and I argued about the best route to get to back from the airport and because I disagreed with her, she refused to speak to me for the rest of the trip. My mother flaunted her new, much younger, boyfriend. She thinks she's gloating and she loves it immensely." The look on her face made his heart sick. "At 'gift-giving time,' she tossed a store bag in my lap and said, '*I wish you'd get yourself a man already so I can stop wasting all this money on you*." She glanced at him and then quickly away. "It's all so completely exhausting." She gathered herself, but he knew she forced that smile onto her face. "I did manage to make it to the beach a couple of times though."

"Did you wear a tiny string bikini?" She would never wear anything like that, but he desperately wanted to make her laugh. Visiting her family was always a trial, and Dean did everything in his power to bring her back from the abyss she sank into whenever she saw them.

Her lips curved, her smile turning more genuine. "Not this time. But I was naked underneath my clothes."

Naked—now there was a pleasant thought. His gaze dropped to the gap in her black wool coat, touched on her bare shoulder, followed the line of her dress over her clavicle, down to the swell of her breasts. Heat rushed to his groin, and he had to clear his throat before he could speak again. "Hot."

"I know."

"What did you do at the beach while not in your bikini?" Her face got animated and his heart was lighter. No matter how much he wanted to, he couldn't take away her pain, he knew that, but he could make her smile.

"I thought about you, actually." She shifted in her seat, and her knee touched his. He knocked her leg playfully aside, and she chuckled, knocking him back. He pressed his knee to hers, and they engaged in a short, violent battle of who could make the other's knee move. She grunted, her butt coming up off the seat with the effort. He laughed as he gave in, letting her win and push his legs aside.

"So, what did you think about when you were thinking about me?" he asked after they settled back down. "Anything good?"

"Very good. 'Member how we talked about that homicidal bunny working in customer service?"

"Of course." He remembered the night well. It was a couple of weeks before Christmas, and they were going to go into the city to check out a new restaurant, but the night was cold and sleeting and they decided to stay in instead. They got a bottle of Jack, camped on his couch, and got drunk off their asses. Somehow they got on the topic of Kat's comics, spitting out ideas for a new series she could write. Some of them were pretty wild, but the bunny was a good one: a deranged rabbit driven to murderous insanity from dealing with the general public. "A great idea."

"I was thinking about what you said and instead of making him an actual serial killer, I think maybe he'd kill them in his mind. He could be a chain-smoking, alcoholic bunny who is as insane and evil as the people who call him. Every episode could be a battle of who is more evil, the complaining, annoying customer or the psycho bunny rep."

Dean nodded, catching her enthusiasm. "That's good. You could give him a regular cast too. A wife, a boss, a drinking buddy." He ran his knuckle along the edge of her thigh. "Maybe even a mistress," he suggested with a wink that made her laugh. "That way it isn't all one-shots."

"You're right." She pointed both of her index fingers at him, and he grinned. They worked well together, their ideas often flowing and meshing naturally, and when things were really good, it was like they could read each other's minds. "And everybody is evil; the most despicable and horrible examples of humanity ever."

He liked the direction this was taking. "They can't all be evil though. There has to be one 'good' character in there; someone to give it balance."

She touched her tongue to her top teeth. "Like a Ned Flanders type?"

"Yeah, but not a joke or a parody. Someone people can actually root for." He searched for the right words. "A despicable antihero can only go so far. You need some light in all that darkness."

She nodded slowly. "A white knight." Her fingertips grazed the back of his hand, sending warmth all the way up to his elbow. "Like you."

She was so achingly beautiful sometimes, she just about killed him. He could easily be in love with her. It was better for them both that he was not. "Am I your white knight?"

"Yes," she said simply, then her smile turned mischievous, her eyes twinkling. "Without you, I'd always wear black."

He laughed and some of the tension dissipated. Or perhaps it had never there at all. It was possible all that electric energy was completely one-sided. He wouldn't put it past himself. Whatever it was, he needed to get over it. "You do always wear black."

"Hmmm, well, maybe you aren't all that good an influence." She squeezed his forearm and then looked away, pressing her fingertips to her lips in a gesture she often made when she was unsure or stressed. "We'll see if I can make it work."

He took her hand and met her eyes. She was an incredible artist, the best graphic artist he'd ever had the pleasure of teaming up with, and her comics were off the charts. "It'll work."

She held his eyes for a long moment and then nodded. "Yeah." She squeezed his hand and then let go. "How about you? How was home?"

"Fantastic." And it had been. He loved seeing his family, spending time with his mom, dad, and brother. A trip home always left him happy and recharged, and this one had come at a particularly good time. It was because of his family's love and support that he was able to be over Mari as quickly as he had and being with them made him realize a lot about his former relationship. Having sex with a model was outrageously good, but hardly the cornerstone of a healthy partnership. There had always been something missing between them, a disconnect of sorts. Seeing his parents together, witnessing how much they loved one another, allowed him to understand that what he'd felt for Marine had been nice, but never truly love. She had come to him for strength and comfort, and he had enjoyed giving it to her. Unfortunately, it wasn't enough.

"Hey." Kat put her hand on his thigh. "She was never worth it,

Dean. She never deserved you."

He gave her a half-smile. Kat disliked Marine from the first day she met her at the photo shoot Ron had commissioned to use for a romance novelist's website. Mari was the perfect waif heroine, delicate and ethereal. She had an air of vulnerability, an innate fragility. She was a woman who wanted to be held, protected, comforted, and he wanted to be the man that got to do it. He asked her out that very night. Their relationship didn't last a full year. "We weren't right for each other, I guess."

"Whatever," she said, and he knew from the tone of her voice that she didn't believe it. "Tell me what you did while you were home."

"Not a whole lot really. We went skiing like every year, and my brother and I did some more planning for our climb of Holy Cross in May." He shrugged one shoulder. "Mostly I ate and relaxed and hung out."

The traffic lurched forward, stopped, lurched again. At this rate, it was going to take forever to get to the West Village. Normally, the delay would drive him nuts, but it had been over a week since he had seen Kat. It was good to catch up with her.

"It sounds great," she said.

"They asked about you." He caught a lock of her hair between his thumb and forefinger and gave it a little tug. "My mom says hi." Ever since his parents visited New York, they asked about Kat. They loved her on sight. "You should come next year."

She sighed. "I'd love to, I would. Your parents are great, but Christmas is my one obligation. It's a pain in the ass, but it's better than dealing with the year-long guilt trip I'd have to endure otherwise, having to hear about how I don't love her enough to go and see her once a year on the most important of family holidays. I'd rather go and get it done."

"Okay," he said, although it wasn't, not at all. "The invitation is always open." He hated what her family did to her, hated the defeat and depression she came back home to New York with every year after a week with those people. There had to be a way for him to shield her from that hurt. Maybe next year he could kidnap her, take her off to Colorado whether she liked it or not. Or even better, he could let her do her obligatory Christmas Eve and day with that god-awful woman and then make her come to Colorado, spend the rest of the holiday break with him. He was certain he could convince her to agree—it would just take some finesse. He thought of how stubborn Kat could be and smiled. Maybe if he started now, he could wear her down by then.

The traffic surged forward as whatever was holding things up cleared out, and they were over the bridge in no time. He leaned back into the seat, listening to the sounds of the city as they wove through lower Manhattan, the rev of truck engines, the squeals of brakes, the snatches of music and screaming and laughter.

He glanced over at the woman at his side, subtly studying her profile. Her blind date was a lucky man. He'd better realize it too. He didn't understand why she agreed to it, but if it was what she wanted to do, he supported her one hundred percent. If the guy turned out to be an asshole, however, well, then, Dean might have to end up having a conversation with him.

He smiled to himself. God, she would hate that. He could imagine the lecture she would give him if he tried to protect her that way. She was going to have to deal with it, though. She knew what she was getting into when she asked him along, it wasn't like they'd just met yesterday.

The cab turned onto Hudson, and he caught a glimpse of a couple locked in a passionate embrace under a streetlamp. The woman's sparkly tiara was askew and the man was missing his shirt, but that didn't seem to deter them one bit. "Why do you think people kiss at midnight?"

She smiled at him. "You get cursed if you don't. If you can't find someone to kiss, all you have to look forward to is bad luck, hairy palms, and failed online dating attempts all year long."

He laughed. "Yeah, everyone knows that, but how do you think it began? I mean, how did it get decided that if you don't kiss someone at midnight, your year is doomed?"

She ran her index finger over her bottom lip as she thought it over. "Well, that whole make-loud-noises-and-be-obnoxious-at-midnight thing is supposed to keep the demons away, so maybe it has something to do with that. Maybe a kiss is a protection as well, a safeguard of some sort, to keep evil away from you in the New Year."

"So, celibacy is evil, then?"

"Some people might argue that it is."

They both laughed. "Maybe demons don't like kissing? That doesn't seem right. You'd think demons would be into anything sexual. More ways to sin, you know?"

"It has to be about more than just sex." She thought for a second and then turned to him, excitement sparkling in her eyes. "Okay, how about this? Kissing is personal. When you kiss, you share another's breath and breath is life, so maybe kissing is an exchange of sorts, like…" Her fingers danced in the air as the ideas formed in her mind. "Like, sharing your soul. Maybe that's what it is. You kiss someone and share a piece of your soul with them. That way they keep it safe for you in the New Year. They have a piece of you inside them." She touched his chest, right over his heart. "Here." Her eyes met his. "Protected." A wicked smile blossomed on her lips and then she shrugged. "Otherwise, it's spinning heads and bad skin for everyone."

"Wow," he said as the cab pulled up in front of Ron and Alan's brownstone. "I'm glad I asked. I would have hated to fuck that up."

She paused from digging around in her coat pockets to nod at him solemnly. "The consequences could have been dire."

He used her distraction to pull his wallet out and pay the driver before she could. She scowled at him, but he only smiled sweetly in return. She despised it when he paid or opened doors for her or did anything like that and it was always a triumph when he got to treat her.

He climbed out of the cab and an icy wind whipped down

Perry Street. The forecast had been calling for snow for days and he thought maybe it was finally coming. Another breeze sliced through his heavy winter coat, and he put his arm around her shoulders to shield her from the cold. They walked up the steps huddled together, and he held her close, the warmth of her body cuddled up against his side. She had such a big personality, such a big presence, he often forgot how small she truly was, how neatly she fit in his arms.

"All right, a kiss at midnight. I'm on it," he said, and pressed the doorbell.

She looked up at him from underneath his arm, her face serious, but her eyes dancing with mischief. "If it's any consolation, I'll call a priest for you if the worst should happen."

"Thank you," he said, matching her mock-earnest tone. Did he imagine that her gaze flicked to his mouth, that for the briefest second, she licked her lower lip? Probably. But it was a damn fine delusion. "I knew I could count on you."

The door swung open, bathing them in a rush of heat and light. Laughter and music floated out, and the distinctive sound of a champagne cork popping made Dean smile. Maybe it was going to be a good night after all. Ron threw the door open wide, grinning broadly as he ushered them inside.

Chapter Two

"Kat!" Ron said, escorting them into his home. Warmth and bright lights greeted them as they entered the foyer. People dotted the Venetian-style living room in pairs and small groups, while tuxedoed waiters passed out glasses of champagne and hors d'oeuvres. Murmured conversations mixed with the snazzy ragtime music, accentuated by the occasional burst of laughter. She and Dean waved to Alan as he passed by with a tray full of festive red martinis.

Ron kissed her on both cheeks, then pivoted on the heel of Gucci loafers to give Dean's hand a hardy shake. "And Dean!" He smiled broadly. "I'm so glad you both came." His gaze shifted between them. Kat caught the speculative twitch of his eyebrow as he took in Marine's absence and Dean's arm around her shoulders. She sighed inwardly. There was always speculation about her and Dean.

Ron loved matchmaking. She suspected that he originally intended for her and Dean to hook up way back when she started with Sharpe Designs and became an official member of the family. On her first day, she should have been placed with another graphic artist, but Ron had sat her next to his golden-boy designer instead. In a way, Ron had achieved another one of his magic pairings. It wasn't the love match she was certain he hoped for, but they did work well together, making some truly unique websites for the eclectic clientele of artists and authors and small businesses

Sharpe Designs catered to. The firm was large enough now to have separate art and production departments, but they still sat next to one another, sharing a small alcove on the top floor of the SoHo office building the company currently occupied.

"So," Ron said, and clapped his hands. "Eric is here."

She could hear the question in his voice, saw in his eyes that he was just waiting for her to confess her undying love for Dean on the threshold of his home and call off the date. Kat grinned to herself. Her boss would love that. He'd probably start drawing up the wedding invitations right on the spot.

"Good," Kat said, and moved away from Dean to remove her coat. She instantly missed his warmth, the comfortable weight of his arm. The lights in the foyer were very bright and her little dress was hardly any protection against the cold. She clenched her jaw and made herself stand taller. She'd faced far worse things than one blind date alone and survived. She didn't need to use him as some kind of crutch.

Ron stood patiently by her side, an encouraging smile on his lips, and a wave of nauseous anticipation made her stomach clench. She couldn't believe she was actually going through with this, that she had become so desperate that she was willing to resort to a blind date of all things. But, silly as it was, it did not stop a small part of her heart from flickering with hope. These last few weeks she had been thinking all kinds of crazy thoughts, things like what it might feel like to not be alone all the time, what it might be like to be held in someone's arms and have it actually mean something. She understood that these things were not meant for people like her; she was far too fucked up in the head and heart to ever have a normal relationship, but the yearning ache would not go away. Kat prided herself on being a woman of action. If she wanted a cure for the unrest, then she needed to do something about it. When Ron presented her with this opportunity, she had jumped at the chance to try something she had never tried before.

She handed her coat to Ron and he passed it off to one of the attendants. "I'm ready," she said as much to herself as to him.

He offered her his elbow. "Eric is dying to meet you, Kat."

She glanced over at Dean, and he nodded toward the right corner of the living room. "I'm going to talk to Shannon."

She followed his gaze over to the very pregnant woman sitting on a maroon overstuffed chair, and she waved to Shannon when their eyes met across the room. Shannon and Dean volunteered for a summer youth program that took disadvantaged children on outdoor adventures all over the city. He loved that program, loved the kids, and he invited her to visit his group several times during the long, hot, sticky summer. She even got to help out once and go kayaking up the Hudson River with them.

She looked back to Dean, ready to bid him farewell, but something tripped in her heart, making her pause. Did she really want to go through all this hassle? Why not ditch the date, the obligation, blow it all off and spend the night with him instead? It would probably be a hell of a lot more fun.

He touched her arm, a light caress that helped quell some of her escalating indecision. "Have your date," he said, his voice pitched low for her ears alone. "Don't worry about me. I have to go return some videotapes."

Laughter exploded out of her, washing away some of her nervous energy, just like he intended. He was such a dork. She poked him in the side and he laughed, dancing away from her. She gave him one last look and took Ron's arm. It was time.

Coworkers greeted her with smiles and nods as Ron paraded her across the living room. He waited until they'd left Dean a short distance behind before asking the question she knew had been burning on his tongue since the moment they walked in the front door. "Where's Marine?"

"Apparently they broke up," she responded, trying to sound as neutral as possible. There was no need for Ron to know how happy that made the selfish little monster within her.

"About time," he muttered, and she smiled. Marine was nobody's favorite person. "Who should we set him up with then? How about our mistress of marketing, Stacy Saunders?"

She shook her head as they approached the bubbly redhead. "I think she might be a bit too wild for him."

Stacy wiggled her fingers at them as they passed, one of those large, fruity cocktails Alan had been passing around in her other hand. Kat's mouth watered. She was ready for drink.

"True," Ron said, sidestepping around one of the many sculpted accent tables. "And he does seem to prefer those wilting, waif girls. Stacy's no damsel in distress."

Kat nodded. That was exactly Dean's type.

"Ah, well, it seems Dean will have to be my project for the New Year." He cut a glance over to Kat. "If he isn't taken by then."

She smiled in spite of herself. "I don't need to be saved either."

"No, of course you don't. Still, it is nice to have someone strong around." His smile brightened as they came to stop before a handsome dark-haired man deep in conversation with a newer member of the extended family, a striking blond woman who owned a recording studio in Queens. They stood close together, their body language clearly indicating that their conversation was intense and private.

"Eric!" Ron said, catching the man's attention.

Kat shot Ron a look that she hoped conveyed her disbelief that Eric had been in fact "dying to meet her," but he pointedly ignored her.

"This is the famous Kathleen Greer I've been telling you about," Ron said, and gave her a small push toward Eric.

The blond gave Ron a tight smile, whispered something quick into Eric's ear, and then walked away without a single backward glance.

Eric watched the woman depart, eyeing her over as she crossed the room, then turned his full attention to Kat. He held out his hand in greeting. "Eric Travo."

He was tall, with olive skin, and hard muscle rippled under his tailored Italian suit. His chocolate-brown eyes were sleepy and hooded, his full lips parted in a sensual smile. He was devastatingly attractive, the kind of man who did ad campaigns for all the top designers, but nothing about him made her insides flutter, not like the way it had been the first time Ron introduced her to Dean. Her insides had done more than flutter that day, the butterflies in her stomach had launched a full-on, Rambo-style assault. If Dean ever had a clue about the initial effect he had on her, she'd be hearing about it to this day. It was a good thing she got over that quickly, especially since he was seeing someone at the time. But then, he was always seeing someone and she was no homewrecker.

"Like I mentioned," Ron said to Eric, "Kat is from California. She's been with Alan and me since she moved to New York and we are lucky to have her. She is one the best graphic artists in the city. Her websites have won some major awards." Kat wanted to amend that, tell Eric those sites were actually partnerships with Dean and the awards were as much his as they were hers, but she kept her mouth shut. Ron would only shush her anyway. "She's also an amazing illustrator and her web comic, *Smoking Razors*, gets..." Ron turned to her, beaming like a proud father. "How much traffic is it getting now, Kat?"

"About eight thousand unique visitors a month." It wasn't a tremendous number, but she was satisfied. More importantly, that number was always increasing.

Eric looked duly impressed, and Ron nodded his approval. He turned to Kat, ready to give her the Eric spiel. Ron did this whenever he introduced people, dropping tidbits of information for conversation starters, creating instant icebreakers. It was part of what made him such a good matchmaker. "Eric was born and raised right here in New York City. He's a freelance writer and photographer, and he's been in *Travel and Leisure*, *GQ*, and *Vanity Fair*. We absolutely want him to do some work for us." He winked at Kat. "I'll leave it to you to convince him."

Kat laughed at Ron's silliness while Eric gave her a longer, more thorough, appraisal. It might not be love at first sight, but the look in his eyes said she could definitely get laid tonight if she wanted to. Strangely, the thought didn't fill her with the kind of anticipation it should have.

Ron grinned happily. "Well," he said, and put his hands on both of their shoulders. "You'll have to excuse me, more guests have arrived, and I must go greet them." He gave their shoulders a light pat and then was gone.

Kat smiled at Eric. The sudden silence was a bit awkward. "So," she said, fumbling for something to fill the void. "A photographer? Are you working on anything interesting?"

Eric's smile turned from polite to genuine. She could see the appeal in those handsome features, the charm. He'd be all about expensive restaurants and long walks through Central Park, bagels and *The Times* on Sunday mornings. Nice, but not anything original. "I'm doing a piece right now on the secret oases of New York."

"Really?" she asked, snagging a glass of champagne from a passing waiter. Nothing in her cared, and she was surprised by the sharp, painful wave of disappointment. Still, she smiled and waited for him to add more. Giving people the freedom to talk about themselves was the best conversational skill she had ever learned. Everyone loved to share their personal philosophies and favorite projects. The technique allowed her to come off as extremely likeable without having to offer any information about herself.

"Yes." He flashed a hundred-watt smile. "There's a whole hidden world you wouldn't expect to find in the city."

Kat cast a quick glance over her shoulder and smiled when she spotted Dean. His hands were on Shannon's stomach, his face alight with joy. Fondness swelled in her heart even as she mentally rolled her eyes. He was such a sucker for all that stuff. He loved to buy into the whole domestic fantasy, the kids, the yard, the golden retriever dream. She bet he'd even install the white picket fence himself if he could. He laughed and though she couldn't hear the sound, she knew it well enough to imagine it clearly. She wanted to go over and see what he was laughing at, join in the merriment. Knowing Dean, it had to be something wickedly fun.

"If you're interested, I could arrange a tour of some of the more private locations," Eric said, drawing her attention back to him by taking a step closer to her.

She sighed. He was sending all the right signals, but this was not how she envisioned the date would go. Somehow, she had gotten it into her head that she was going to have some kind of magical revelation tonight and that was simply not the case.

"There's this little beach out in the Rockaways I think you'll like. It's impossible to find if you don't already know it's there. Spectacular view." He paused, met her gaze. "It's beautiful, like you."

The flattery was nice, but unimpressive. She made a token noncommittal noise and downed half of her champagne. She was not ready to give up yet. If this was going to work, then she was going to have to put forth a real effort. She straightened her spine and gave him a wide smile. This date was going to be a success, dammit.

Eric grinned. He obviously thought she was caught in his snare of seduction. Kat smiled to herself, liking the turn of phrase—snare of seduction. She pictured a giant spider web and a woman with huge breasts and minimal clothing tangled in the net. She could feel the presence of the predator in her mind, see him hovering in the distance, the dark, seductive weight of his stare as he watched his latest conquest writhe helplessly in his trap.

"I'd show you things that'd make you purr, Kitty-Kat," Eric said, breaking once more into her thoughts.

Kat winced inwardly, but forced herself to laugh. It came out a little too loud, a little too boisterous, but it was the best she could do.

He reached out and ran his knuckles down her bare arm, a move clearly designed to see if she was receptive to his touch. Bitterness pricked her heart. When had she become so cynical? She wasn't all that touchy-feely by nature. The only person she allowed to touch her on regular basis was Dean, but this was different. This was supposed to about romance—or at the very least sex. She should be laughing, having fun. This incredibly attractive man wanted to sleep with her and that was not something to be upset about. And yet she was. She had hoped for something new and this was just more of the same.

Eric traced her wrist. "That's quite a tat," he said, dropping his voice an octave to a velvety rumble. "What's it mean?"

"It's just a quote." She waved her hand in dismissal. She didn't want to share that story with him. It was a little too personal for a casual anecdote. The tattoo had been another impulsive decision, much like agreeing to this blind date. She and Dean had been eating lunch at their desks one afternoon, her mind wandering as she tore into her Cubano sandwich. She couldn't even imagine what was going on in the apartment across the way, but there was a huge Cheshire-cat grin painted on their window. That grin made her unbelievably happy and she turned to him and said, "I think I want to get a tattoo that says, 'We're all mad here.'" He looked up from his skinless, boneless, broiled chicken breast, smiled, and said, "You must be or you wouldn't have come here." She was pretty sure that was the exact moment he became her best friend in the whole world.

"It's great work," Eric said, giving her a brilliant-white lady-killer smile.

"Thanks," she said, and though she didn't really want to, she continued to play the game, looking up at him through her lashes. Ron was right as usual. Eric was perfect for her, but not in the way Ron had intended when he arranged this date. Eric was purely out for a good time—no promises, no obligations. He was exactly the type of man she always pursued. She could easily begin a relationship with him and like with every other man she'd dated, she could see him, have sex, and then go back to her quiet life. He would never ask for anything more from her.

But really, what did she expect? Love, kisses, promises of

eternity? She snorted softly and took another sip of champagne. Hell, she was lucky if she got a phone call the next day. Those were unrealistic expectations. And she should have known better.

Eric spoke, probably telling her something witty or clever, but the words were distant and unfocused. Her gaze drifted to his lips, and the thought of kissing him at midnight, of sharing her soul with him, made her sad. She pushed the idiotic emotion away, cursing her own hyper-romantic imagination. It was just a kiss. It didn't mean anything. For a self-proclaimed realist, she harbored a lot of crazy ideas. But now that the thought was there, she couldn't quite shake it.

"We could take my Motobeast and get away for a while."

Eric's light touch on her shoulder snapped her attention back. She tried to make sense of what he'd said, but all she could do was blink in confusion. "I'm sorry, what?"

"My Motobeast. My bike." He moved into her personal space, and she fought the urge to back up. "I know this trail up in Inwood, way past the GW Bridge. Really secluded. I'd love to take you for a ride."

It took a minute, but the fact that he had seriously offered to give her "a ride" sunk in and she had to bite back the giggles that threatened to explode out of her mouth. What a disaster. She should have stayed home.

Another helpful New Year's resolution occurred to her: Don't accept rides from strange men. At this rate, she was going to have a full list by the end of the night.

* * * * *

Dean watched Kat walk away with Ron, mesmerized by the sway of her hips. Every step she took caused her short, sparkly dress to flip up a little bit, showing off her toned thighs. A part of him that didn't give a damn about friendship fiercely hoped that it would flip up a tiny bit higher. When it granted his wish, the flash of long legs and nylons, the hint of her garter, left him breathless.

He took a step forward, his hand extended, but stopped himself. It wouldn't be fair to call her back, no matter how much it burned him up to watch her walk off to another man. She shrugged the date off in the cab, but they both knew that no one let Ron mess around with their love life unless they were serious about finding someone. This date was a huge opportunity for her and a gigantic step forward. He was happy for her. Really. Maybe if he told himself that enough times, he might begin to believe it.

He tore his gaze away from Kat and commanded himself to walk over to Shannon. He'd introduced Shannon to Ron and Alan about a year ago at a fundraiser for Urban Adventures, the inner-city youth program they both volunteered with. Ron and Alan loved her so much they instantly welcomed her and her husband, Mike, into the mishmash of relatives, friends, lovers, and associates that comprised the Sharpe Designs Extended Family. The last time he'd seen her was the end of August, when they'd finished up another summer. He was glad she was at the party.

She was very round now, and it probably wasn't much longer before she was due. She looked uncomfortable, but she was practically glowing, her face a radiant light in the crowded living room. He hugged her hello, the baby a delightful mound between them.

"How have you been?" she asked, hugging him back.

"Good." He hovered over her, trying not to appear too anxious. His fingers itched to touch her, but he didn't want to be rude. "Is she kicking tonight?"

"Here," Shannon said, and took his hand, placing it under her left breast. There was a flutter and then a rock-solid kick under his palm.

"She's strong!" He smiled in pure delight. "Just like her mom." The baby kicked again and Dean's smile grew wider. "Maybe you'll have a New Year's baby."

"I don't think she's coming tonight, but I'll tell you what, the sooner the better," Shannon said with a groan. "I am so ready."

He laughed, loving the feel of the baby under his palm. He wanted lots of kids of his own.

Kat's laughter caught his attention and he looked over in her direction. It sounded louder than usual, forced. He frowned. There was something about the stiffness in her neck, the set of her shoulders, that made his chest tighten. It might be time for him to go over and make sure everything was all right.

"She looks very beautiful," Shannon said, flashing him a puckish grin. Her gaze cut over to Kat and then back to him, so there was no mistaking who she was talking about.

"Yeah, she does," he agreed, straightening up. Kat was going to be fine. He rubbed his side, where she poked him earlier. She was small, but she was strong. He didn't want to get poked again. If he went over there and butted in where he wasn't wanted, he was sure to get that and a whole lot more. A waiter approached with a tray of champagne and he grabbed a glass. He'd let it be—for now.

"Who's the guy?" she asked, blatantly checking out Kat's blind date.

He shrugged. "Someone Ron set her up with." He took a sip of champagne and his gaze drifted back to Kat.

"I never understood why you two don't get together," she said, eyeing him up and down.

Dean shook his head. People couldn't seem to understand their relationship. "Kat and I are friends."

Shannon raised her eyebrows. "Mike and I are friends too."

"It's not like that." It had never been like that. From the minute she sat down next to him and wowed him with her total graphic overhaul of a website he had been struggling with for days, they had been friends. Sure, he'd allowed himself a few harmless fantasies about her. He worked with her every day, saw her most weekends. He'd seen every mood she had, been beside her when she was happy and sad, excited, crabby, frustrated, disappointed, elated, bemused. It was only natural that he be curious about what she might look like when she was aroused, to wonder what expression might be on her pretty face when he touched her, to dream about what might happen after he found her wet and yielding. But it didn't mean anything. It never went beyond the realm of his imagination. "And honestly, I probably flirt with you more than I flirt with Kat."

She smiled up at him. "And if I wasn't married, I'd totally sleep with you."

He jerked, spilling half his glass of champagne. "What?"

"Oh, Dean, don't be naïve. You know exactly how attractive you are. And I've seen you in a swimsuit." Her eyes flicked to his crotch. "I know what you have to offer."

He couldn't help but laugh. "You're kidding."

"Not even a little."

He took a step back and allowed himself to look at her as a woman rather than as his very married co-counselor. She was about ten years older than he was, with short, dark hair, and a pleasant oval face. When not pregnant, her body was normally fit and lean, a true swimmer's build. She was attractive and he really liked her smile, the way it lit up her entire face. She had the kind of smile that made everyone around her want to smile too. She wasn't his usual type, but he supposed he might sleep with her if things were different. His gaze slid over to Kat. Maybe sleeping with a friend wasn't such a bad idea.

"See," she said, wagging her finger at him. "You're thinking about it, which proves my point."

His cheeks heated. "Yeah, but—"

"I know, you're friends. I get it. I'm just saying that sometimes friendships can become something more." She smiled over at her husband, who was talking to a group of people by the snack tables. "Especially the really good ones."

He couldn't come up with a viable argument against that and shrugged instead. However reasonable it may be, he and Kat were never going to go there. They didn't want the same things from a relationship.

Shannon flashed him a grin he couldn't quite interpret and made a point of looking around the room. "Where's Marine?"

"We broke up." He was surprised at how casually he could say it, how little pain he felt. Things had been less than ideal between them for some time, and now that it was over, he was glad to be free.

She touched his wrist. "I'm sorry."

"It's okay." And it was. Mari would never have wanted to go to this party. She would have insisted on going to Tilt or some equally hip club and spent the entire night trying to get in front of as many cameras as possible. Dean encouraged her ambition, admired it, but it was tiring. It was a relief to not have to deal with it anymore, to be able to spend a quiet New Year's Eve with friends instead.

He glanced over at Kat and noted that the guy had moved much closer to her. Maybe she was having a good time. He was glad. This date could be a really positive thing for her. She spent way too much time alone. Still, he'd hoped to hang out with her more tonight, maybe even sneak off and get a peek at the ginormous, spectacular new jacuzzi Ron and Alan couldn't stop bragging about. He grinned to himself. That actually sounded like a pretty good idea. He was definitely going to have to grab her later for that excursion.

"You'll be fine," Shannon said.

It took him a moment to reconnect the dots of their conversation. Marine. Of course. "Yeah," he said, waving it away. He would be fine.

"Wife," Shannon's husband Mike said, sliding up alongside her chair.

Her eyes lit up with unmistakable happiness. "Husband," she answered, reaching for him to kiss her.

Dean smiled. They had such a great marriage. He could feel the warmth in the way they looked at one another and he envied it a bit. Marine had never looked at him like that, but to be fair, he'd never looked at her like that either. He wanted to look at someone like that, though, and have her look back at him. Kat would say that made him a sap, but he didn't care.

He turned away when they kissed again. Was he ever going to find that kind of love? He hoped so, he wanted it, but this latest breakup in his long line of breakups really made him wonder. Mike and Shannon proved it was out there. Why was he having so much trouble finding it?

He snuck another glance at Kat and watched as she lifted her right leg and rotated her ankle. She shifted her weight and then did the same thing with her left foot. He frowned. He'd seen that rolling ankle many times, at countless meetings and cocktail parties; anytime she was bored, restless or wanting to be somewhere else. It could be nothing, but he didn't think so. He should check. Just to make sure. If it was nothing, that was fine, but if she needed him, he wanted to be there.

He smiled at Shannon and Mike. "Excuse me," he said, and left them to go check on his friend.

Chapter Three

Kat finished her champagne and rolled her ankle around while she searched for another waiter. She was going to get shitfaced drunk tonight, she decided, righteously fucked-up; then she was going to sleep with Eric and ring in the New Year with a motherfucking bang. If she had to settle, then she was going to do it in style. She just needed some more alcohol.

She caught a waiter's eye and was about to commence on her mission when a hand fell on her shoulder. Her head jerked to the right and she blinked, surprised to find Dean beside her. "Kat," he said. His face was serious, but his eyes held an impish light.

"Hello, Dean." She gave him a questioning look, but he just smiled. Curious. "Eric, this is Dean Kirkwell."

The men nodded to one another and Dean's hand skimmed down the back of her arm to hold her elbow. "I know this is probably a bad time," he said, trying to look apologetic, but failing miserably. "And I hate to interrupt, but I saw you over here and I had to take the chance. I have a really important question about the Fisher account. It's quick, I swear." He looked from her, to Eric, back to her again. "But I completely understand if you can't do it right now."

Kat wanted to laugh out loud. He was saving her. And even worse, she was actually grateful. He did it so smoothly too, leaving it open for her to say yes or no. The decision was entirely hers. She could stay with Eric, have some righteous New Year's sex, and maybe enjoy an encore or two after that, but the whole thing would be over by Spring. Or, she could hang out with Dean.

"I'm sorry," she said, turning to Eric. She tried to put on her most regretful face. She didn't want to be mean or offend him, but it was not working for her. "Do you mind? This project is important."

Dean let go of her elbow and moved his hand to her lower back. He met Eric's gaze over the top of her head and something passed between them, something tense and very male. She scowled, pissed off by the posturing, but they ignored her.

It passed quickly and Eric looked from Dean to Kat. "Of course," he said, his voice betraying the insincerity of his smile. "He obviously needs you very badly."

Dean's smile showed lots of teeth. "I do."

Kat sighed. This was not what she wanted. "Thanks," she said, mostly because she couldn't think of anything else to say.

Eric nodded and she allowed Dean to guide her away. Once they got to an isolated corner on the other side of the room, he pulled two glasses off a passing waiter's tray and handed one to her. She downed it instantly and then traded her empty glass for a full one before the man could walk away.

Dean eyed her closely. "It's like that, huh?"

"He wanted to show me his Motobeast." It seemed to sum up the entire craptastic night perfectly.

His face went completely blank for a split second, then he started to laugh. "What?"

"His Motobeast. His bike."

"Right," he said, and his amusement only annoyed her more. "His bike."

The look on his face made her want to laugh and laughing was the last thing she wanted to do. She elbowed him in the gut. "You're not helping."

He leaned down close to her, a wicked smile on his lips. "Did he offer to *give you a ride?*"

When she didn't answer, his eyes widened in absolute glee and a tremendous grin broke out on his handsome face. He threw his arm around her shoulders and laughed into her hair to muffle the sound. The vibrations of his laughter rippled through Kat, tickling her insides, making her want to giggle. She put her hand on his chest, trying to make him stop before he could completely infect her. She was trying to be upset, dammit. Her New Year's was ruined. "Cut it out." She ground her teeth, but the merriment was bubbling inside. "It's not funny."

He only laughed harder and then pressed his mouth against her ear. "Hey, little girl, I've got some candy in my pocket." His voice was low and teasing, a deep rumble that sent chills down her arms. "It's not a ride, but it is very sweet."

"Dean!" But she was laughing too hard to put any force behind it.

He gave her a quick hug. "You're welcome, by the way," he said, flashing her a smug grin.

Kat rolled her eyes. "Yeah, well, don't go breaking your arm patting yourself on the back. I was fine."

"Sure."

She grunted and shook her head. There was no use arguing. She shot a quick glance back over at Eric and spotted him in deep conversation with the blond once more. The woman said something that made Eric smile and Kat tried not to be bitter with her own failure. If she had stuck it out, all it would have amounted to was another notch in her tired old bedpost. She'd wanted more from tonight. She supposed she was grateful for Dean's intervention, but all she felt was weary defeat.

Dean caught the direction of her stare. He must have seen something in her face because he put his arm back around her shoulders. "Come on," he said, turning her away from the scene. "Let's go sit down somewhere."

The apartment was filled with laughter and revelry and there were people everywhere: on the chairs, the sofas, even perched on the accent tables. They wove through the living room, stopping occasionally to chat with friends and coworkers as they searched for some space. They eventually made their way down the long hallway toward the bathroom and found an empty guest bedroom. Kat walked in and flopped down on the bed.

He sat beside her and laid back, his hands laced behind his head. His shirt rode up, exposing his flat stomach, the line of golden-brown hair that started below his navel and then disappeared down into his jeans. He had the kind of stomach that was made for licking—taut and firm, with those sexy square blocks of hard abdominal muscle. Her eyes began to trace the path, but she tore her gaze away before she could follow it too far. Sometimes he was too damn gorgeous for his own good.

"Why'd you do it?" he asked, looking up at the ceiling.

She looked down at her hands. A million answers occurred to her, a million reasons and explanations, but at the core of it all, there was only one truth. "Sometimes I get so lonely."

She straightened her spine, ready for the jokes and teasing, but he remained quiet. She glanced back at him over her shoulder and met his solemn gaze. He nodded to her, a silent acknowledgment of total understanding.

She nodded back and then returned her gaze to her lap. Well, this night was a bust. She probably should have tried harder with Eric, done something different. There must have been some way she could have made it work. Granted, Eric was not her prince charming, but it wasn't really about him. It was about the damned hope she allowed herself to be suckered in by every single time. Was she ever going to learn? She pressed her fingertips to her lips and strove for the coldness that was her constant companion, the emotional void that was so much better than the churning disappointment.

The bed creaked when Dean sat up, and she was surprised when he wrapped his arms around her, hugging her from behind. His warmth flooded over her as he gently cradled her, and it was so easy to let go, to relax and accept the comfort, the strength that he offered. Tension drained out of her muscles, and she closed her eyes, safe in his arms. A small part of her whispered that maybe this is what it meant to be held by someone and have it mean something. She liked the thought that it might be true.

A roaring cry from the party outside startled them both, and Kat glanced toward the closed bedroom door. She caught snatches of excited conversation, heard the rumblings of people getting into place, finding partners to ring in the New Year. "Two minutes!" a man yelled. Someone whistled and multiple champagne corks popped at once.

She patted the backs of Dean's hands and sighed. "Looks like we fail. I wonder if there's an exorcism app we can download?"

He chuckled and gave her a playful squeeze. "We could kiss each other."

A spark of interest, of heat, ignited her blood, but she quickly squashed it. He was messing with her as usual. He almost had her that time, though. If he knew how close she had come to falling for it, he'd never let her live it down. She snorted out a laugh and shook her head. "I don't want your cooties."

"Would it be so terrible?" he asked, curling his fingers into hers. He ran his thumbs over her knuckles and a strange feeling gathered in her chest. Not a bad feeling, just foreign, and kind of exciting. "I mean, it couldn't be worse than that time you puked on me, right?"

She groaned, remembering the night she wished to her bones she could forget. That disaster had been entirely his fault. She told him she didn't do well with sweet shots. "I don't know, that was pretty awesome, and I seem to recall you laughing the whole time."

"Yeah," he said, laughing even now. "It was funny." He shifted her in his arms so they faced one another. "Come on, Kat. One kiss." He flashed her a lighthearted grin. "I'll keep your soul safe."

He placed his hand over his heart. "I promise."

He was teasing her, but there was more there; a hint of something deeper in his eyes. The air crackled between them; an erotic tension that made her skin tingle. Her gaze flicked to his mouth. A hot twinge vibrated deep in her core. Was she actually going to kiss him? Exhilarating fear shot along her nerve endings, quickening her pulse.

There was a loud cheer and they both looked toward the door as the countdown began. Only seconds remained. She met his eyes and a shiver traveled from the top of her head, right down to her pinky toes. Like he said, it was just one kiss. What could it hurt? "I never did like pea soup."

He smiled and dipped his head as the commotion grew louder. His lips drew nearer and her breath hitched.

"FOUR...THREE...TWO..."

Their noses bumped and they laughed and then his mouth was on hers. He touched her face, his thumb stroking her cheek as he caught her upper lip between both of his. There was a spark, an instant jolt, and rippling shockwaves washed over her. The outside world vanished and there was only Dean. His kiss. His tongue touched the corner of her mouth, hesitant at first and then bolder, tracing her lower lip. She opened for him and when his tongue slipped inside, electricity rocketed down her spine. He tasted of warmth and champagne, and something else too, something so deliriously good, Kat's head swam from the force of it.

She kissed him hard, hungrily, meeting his mouth again and again, until she ran out of air, until she had no choice but to pull back or die from asphyxiation. She was panting as they parted, her heart racing. She tried to retreat, give herself some space to process what she had just done, but his arms tightened around her, holding her still.

"Kat," he murmured, and then took her mouth again.

There was no time to think, only act, and she gave him more than she had ever given a kiss before, everything she had ever longed to share with another person. This was the kiss she had always secretly dreamed about, the fairytale-princess kiss that swept everything away and left wonder in its wake. A magic kiss. She stroked his back, his powerful muscles flexing under her fingertips, the kiss escalating with every touch of their tongues, every playful dart, every nip and sigh. His fingers tangled in her hair and he drew her tightly against him, intensifying their connection. She relaxed her jaw, letting him in, letting him take everything he wanted. He cupped the back of her head, let out a low growl, and thrust his tongue deep into her mouth.

A door slammed like a shotgun blast and they jumped back from one another.

"Dean!" a woman bellowed. Her French accent was unmistakable. Kat groaned when she opened her eyes and found Marine in the room.

Marine's eyes flicked from Dean to Kat and then back to Dean. She raised one professionally sculpted eyebrow and waited.

Kat's head reeled from the kiss; she was dizzy, lightheaded, her insides buzzing. She wanted Dean again, his mouth on hers, his hands on her body. She loathed Marine at the best of times and right now she wanted to punch the woman in the throat.

"Mari," Dean said, his face the picture of shock and confusion. "What are you doing here?"

"What am I doing here?" Marine demanded. "I catch you cheating on me and all you can say is, what are you doing here?"

He looked to Kat and she could see that he was as dazed as she was. He shook his head and then looked back at Marine. "We broke up."

"Dean," Marine said, the whine in her voice making Kat's head ring. "We had a misunderstanding."

He shook his head again. The hazy look faded away, morphing into what Kat recognized as anger. "I didn't misunderstand anything."

"But," Marine moaned, flinging herself at him. He stood up

to catch her and she buried her head against his chest. When she spoke, her voice was muffled and teary. "I came here for you. I need you, *mon aimé.*"

The entire scene was making Kat sick for far too many reasons. Her heart thudded, her blood racing with adrenalin and arousal. She needed to get away from them, away from her own outrageously conflicting emotions. She looked around, but there was no escape. They were blocking the exit.

Dean extracted himself from Marine's clutches and put some space between them. "You were the one who left, Marine. You were the one who said we were done. You can't have it both ways."

Marine's gorgeous face contorted and Kat was taken aback by her savage display of anger. "I knew," she said, spewing venom and rage. "I knew you were cheating with her!" She pushed him back. "I have told you and told you that she wants you, and the first time I go away, there she is—"

"Hey," he said, breaking into her tirade. "Kat has nothing to—"

Marine let out a sharp scream and stabbed his chest with her index finger. "Well, guess what, Dean! While you were with your *friend*," she gave the word extra special rancor, "I was sleeping with Ross the entire time we were in Calais over Christmas." Her grin was feral and her small, white teeth glinted in the low light. "He got me the best editorial spread of my entire career. What have you ever done for me?"

For a heartbeat everyone froze, and Marine's words reverberated in the silent room.

Fury washed over Kat in a red haze. "You bitch!" she snarled, and leapt to her feet, ready to tear Marine's heart out.

Dean's arm shot out, blocking her advance. He never took his eyes from Marine. "What?"

His voice was so eerily calm. Cold. Dean was never cold. One of the best things about him was his warmth, the easy way he opened up to people and gave them his heart. She was the one who blocked people out, she was the one who didn't trust, she was the one who did her best not to feel. She didn't want that for him. This woman was not worth it. She curled her hands around his forearm, gripping him tightly, giving him every ounce of strength and support she could muster.

Marine realized her mistake and her eyes instantly turned big and wet, her lower lip trembled. If Kat didn't hate the woman as much as she did, she might have respected the sudden, total transformation. It was truly Oscar caliber. "It was for the job. H-he *made* me, and I thought you left me. I was lonely and…" She pawed at his shirt, but he brushed her hands aside.

"Get out." His voice was deadly quiet.

"Dean," she whimpered.

Something passed over him and his face softened, the harsh lines of brutal anger slowly ebbing away. He let out a long breath. "Go, Marine. It's over."

Kat watched him let go of his rage and she ached for him. She wished there was some way she could take his pain, do something more than stand impotently by his side. He was a good man, far too good for Marine. He didn't deserve to have his heart broken.

Marine lifted her chin and curled her upper lip. "Do not call me ever again." She spun on her heel and flounced out of the room. The door banged shut behind her.

They were quiet in the wake of her exit, both of them staring at the closed bedroom door.

"Dean…" Kat began, but everything she could think of to say seemed trite and clichéd. So instead, she wrapped her arms around his waist and hugged him tight.

"It's okay." He rested his chin on top of her head and hugged her back. "It was over way before tonight."

She looked up into his eyes. "You know, I can think of several excellent places to hide a dead body right here in Manhattan."

The lead weight lifted from her chest when he laughed. "I bet you can," he said and tightened his arms around her.

She rested her cheek against his chest, listened to the sound of his heart. "What did you ever see in her?"

"She had ambition. Goals. I didn't always like her methods, but she always knew what she wanted. I respected that." He shrugged. "And she needed me."

"She never needed you. That true love that you want so badly has nothing to do with 'need.' I mean, look at you. You're completely over her. I'd like to think love wouldn't fade so fast."

"You're right," he said, and she was surprised he agreed. She gathered him closer when he pressed his lips into her hair. "I thought about marrying her."

Kat's stomach clenched. "Tell me you're joking."

He shook his head. "She was everything I thought I wanted. When we talked about the future, it always revolved around having a family."

She rolled her eyes. "What she wanted was a meal ticket."

"Yeah, I know," he said. "But I would have considered it a fair trade."

She put her hand against his chest and pushed him back just enough to look up into his face. "Why?"

"Because I was afraid there was nothing else."

She thought of Eric. "Is there anything else?"

He held her gaze. "Yes."

The word hung in the air between them. She became very aware of the pressure of his hips against hers, the heat of his body. Her gaze fell to his lips, lingering there. Dangerous thoughts made her temperature rise.

He dipped his head, a slow desent that quickened her pulse and bought his mouth close to hers. She tasted his breath, inhaled his scent. Her eyes drifted shut and his lips brushed hers, once, but then he was gone, jumping back as yet another person barged into the room.

"Oh!" Stacy blurted out as she fell through the open door, some of her festive red Martini sloshing onto the hardwood floor. Her eyebrows furrowed when she managed to right herself. "This isn't the bathroom."

Kat gritted her teeth. She was going to murder the next person who crossed that threshold. "It's two doors down."

Stacy looked at her, at Dean, at the bed behind them. A sly smile blossomed on her lips. "Well, now, have you two been doing something naughty?"

"No," Kat said, and even to her own ears it sounded defensive. "Don't be silly."

Stacy eyed her suspiciously. "Does that mean your date is up for grabs?"

Kat suppressed a shudder. "He's all yours if you want him."

Her grin grew wider. "I knew it!"

"That doesn't mean anything," Dean said. "I'm way better company."

"Huh-uh," Stacy said. She stood up on her tiptoes, getting up close to his face. "Is that why your cheeks are all rosy?"

He backed away from her intense scrutiny. "Come on, Stace—"

"Let me be the first to say—*it's about damn time, you guys!*" She made an attempt at a sad face, but her persistent smile destroyed the intended effect. "Though it is something of a shame. You were next on my list, Dean."

He blinked. "Ahhh…" He looked from Kat to Stacy, back to Kat. "Thanks?"

Stacy sighed dramatically. "You are such a cutie."

"Okay," Kat said, stepping right into the middle of that mess. The things she did for Dean sometimes. "How many of those Martinis have you had?"

"Three, five, who knows?" Stacy said, waving it all away. "What matters is that it's after midnight and I'm still looking for my kiss."

She put her arm though Dean's. A midnight kiss was special. She had never really known that before. "You'll find it."

Kat thought she might have seen a hint of moisture in Stacy's eyes. "Maybe next year." The melancholy did not last long. She brightened almost instantly and grabbed Kat by the shoulders.

"Happy New Year!" she bellowed, and gave Kat a loud, smacking kiss on the cheek, then spun on her heel and similarity accosted Dean.

"Happy New Year," they both replied.

"All right, I'm off," Stacy said, and downed the last of her cocktail. "Don't worry, I'll let you guys deliver the good news to everyone on Monday." Her grin returned in full force. "Wish me luck. The night's not over yet!"

"Good luck," Kat said.

Stacy wiggled her fingers at them, then turned and sauntered out of the room.

Dean put his arm around Kat's shoulders. "Wow."

Kat laughed softly. "Yeah." There was a tremendous bang as another door crashed open farther down the hall. "I hope she finds her kiss."

"She will." He gave her a little nudge. "Let's get out of here."

She nodded and allowed Dean to lead her out of the room.

They found Ron and Alan snuggled together by the fireplace and said their good-byes, exchanged kisses and New Year's greetings, and promised to catch up on everything on Monday. Kat linked her arm through Dean's and they left the brownstone, huddling together against the cold. Fortunately, they found a cab back to Brooklyn as soon as they reached the avenue.

He was uncharacteristically quiet on the way home and Kat left him alone with his thoughts. She also needed some time to think. Maybe not think, exactly, maybe all she really needed was a cold shower. His kiss was fresh in her mind, and her fingers itched to touch him again, to feel all that hard muscle under her palms. She licked her lower lip and the faint taste of him sent a jolt of lust rocketing through her system.

She clenched her thighs together and fought against the heat that wanted to settle deep between them. She needed to stop. It was just a kiss, nothing earth-shattering. And what she felt—that crazy, wonderful feeling that she'd felt—well, she'd had a lot of champagne and for some reason she was far too imaginative tonight.

She snuck a quick glance at him and her eyes immediately dropped to his lips. Her thighs twitched. Raw desire barreled over her, heating her cheeks, chest, stomach. She always knew he'd be good in bed, but his kiss surpassed even her best fantasies. It was the perfect mix of gentle and aggressive, demanding, but soft. She had no doubt he could do things with his tongue to make a girl scream.

The cab came to a halt in front of her brownstone, and she looked away from him. Just in time too. Any longer in that close, dim space, and she might have done something regrettable.

The cold slapped her in the face as soon as she stepped out of the vehicle, but Dean was quickly there beside her, shielding her from the worst of it. She burrowed into him, taking full advantage of his warmth as they rushed up her front steps. A full-body tremor ran over her when they entered her apartment, the heat tightening her skin. They laughed and shivered out the last of the cold as they stripped off their jackets, scarves, gloves, and hung them on the coat rack by the door.

He plopped down on the couch while she went to the kitchen to find something to drink. She could have sworn she had a whole fifth of Jack somewhere, but she rifled through every single cabinet and only found one nearly empty bottle. Had they really drank that much the last time he was over?

She grabbed the bottle and went back to the living room. He was in his favorite position, stretched out on her couch, his feet up on her coffee table. She opened the whiskey, swigged about half of it, then handed him the rest. He drained it in one gulp.

She gave the empty bottle a longing glance, sat down, and reached over his shins for the remote. The television came alive with images of balloons and ancient rock stars, people kissing passionately as metallic confetti rained down upon them.

"Hey," he said, and touched the back of her neck. His light

caress made her shiver. She looked at him over her shoulder and when their eyes met, she smiled, the soft heat of tender affection radiating in her chest. Platonic affection. He held his arm open to her. "Come here."

She settled in beside him and he draped his arm around her shoulders. Street noise filtered in, melding with the TV, a quiet cacophony of traffic and drunken people, fireworks and music. Wind rattled the windows, a portent of the storm to come.

Kat rested her head against his chest. What a night. Eric. Marine. She was so glad it was finally over. She placed her hand over his heart, its steady beat strong beneath her fingertips. He combed his fingers through her hair: a long, sensual stroke that made her scalp tingle. A twinge of arousal blipped in her veins, but she quickly squashed it. Kissing time was over. She was just hanging out with Dean—like always.

He shifted and the friction of his clothing against her bare flesh sent chills racing along her nerve endings. The gentle stroke of his fingers changed, transformed from something soothing into an intensely erotic caress. Heat pulsed deep in her belly, and Kat became acutely aware of the warmth of his body, the clean scent of his skin. Their eyes met and electricity scorched the air between them.

"I want to kiss you so badly," he said, his normally rich voice husky and raw. He dipped his head, his mouth hovering over hers, his breath on her lips.

A five-thousand-ton anvil of arousal dropped straight to her core. "What's stopping you?"

His gaze flicked from her eyes to her mouth, back to her eyes. "It's not weird for you?"

"I guess it should be, huh?" She searched her heart, trying to give a name to what this was. It was definitely not weird. It was nerve-wracking and exciting, exhilarating, but strangely enough, natural. "It's not, though." She lifted her chin, offering him everything. "I like it."

He stole a quick kiss. "I like it too."

She kissed him back, enjoying the tease. "It isn't anything like I imagined."

A wide grin broke out on his handsome face. Damn, but he could be breathtaking sometimes. "You imagined this? Us?"

"I've thought about what it might be like…" She paused. Maybe it wasn't a good idea to tell him all the things she'd thought about, that some nights she'd lie awake in bed, imagining what it might be like to be in his arms, to have the weight of his body on top of hers, to feel the texture of his tongue against her softest, most intimate parts. Her cheeks flushed from embarrassment and arousal. "To kiss you."

"Yeah?" he asked, his eyes gleaming with pure delight. He nuzzled her nose, his lips ghosting over hers. Liquid heat spiraled through her and her thigh muscles tensed. "What else did you think about?"

She smiled and shook her head. He wasn't going to get it out of her that easily. "You've never thought about it?"

"Oh, I've thought about it." He traced the side of her face, her neck, a tingling, feather-light touch that strummed the heat building in her veins. He lingered over the hollow of her throat, lightly stoking her hypersensitive skin, then dragged his fingers down to rest right above her cleavage. The weight of his gaze on her breasts made her nipples perk in reply. He looked up, directly into her eyes. "About a lot more than just kissing."

Kat swallowed hard. "Oh?" Her heart jack-hammered. She wondered if he could feel it. "Like what?"

Dean's eyes went dark. "Let me show you."

He took her mouth slowly, thoroughly, kissing her until her toes curled in her platform shoes. The touch of his mouth, his lips, his tongue, made her insides sommersault, made her hot and chilled and hungry at the same time. Her fingers tangled in his silky, thick hair, and she breathed him in.

He nipped her lower lip, then flicked his tongue hard into her mouth. She laughed, delirious, punch-drunk, her body buzzing with desire. The insane had occurred—she was making out with Dean. And it was incredible. She pulled her chin back, teasing him, making him chase her. They parted and met and parted again, their kisses sweet, passionate, and more than a little aggressive.

He held her gaze and kissed her once, twice, three times more, and then cupped her breast. She gasped when he gave her a gentle squeeze. Her body burned, craving him, and her nipples peaked, achingly sensitive against the fabric of her bra. She pulled his mouth to hers and the kiss they shared next was all raw, hot sex.

She caressed his neck, his collarbone, and then unbuttoned the top two buttons on his shirt. Dean had a great body, she'd seen him with his shirt off enough times to know that, but touching him was another experience entirely. His skin was soft, smooth, the muscle beneath toned and rock hard. She unhooked another button, greedy for more, and pushed his shirt aside to explore the broad expanse of his chest. He nibbled his way to her neck, and gave her throat one, long lick. Lust rolled over her when he bit down on her earlobe. She nuzzled his jaw, giving him wet, open-mouthed kisses in between gasping sighs. Her body beat a fierce, drumming command deep in her core. Every touch was electric, amplified to the thousandth degree. Her hand glided farther down his chest, the light hair tickling her fingertips. He moaned when she plucked his nipple, a deep rumble that vibrated right down to her already-slick folds. She tweaked it again to hear him moan some more.

"Don't ever stop doing that." He gasped when she scraped her nail lightly over the hard peak.

She smiled. Turning him on was a lot of fun. "Good?" She rolled his nipple between her fingertips, lightly squeezing.

"Oh, yeah," he breathed out.

"How about this?" She kissed his collarbone and then dragged her tongue down his chest. He twitched when she took his nipple into her mouth, shuddering when she sucked on him.

His low groans gave her oodles of shivery delight, and she teased him until he gripped her hair in his fists and dragged her mouth back to his. Their lips met, and she opened for him, letting him take all that he wanted.

The kiss grew, intensified, and he bit down on her lower lip as he pulled her onto his lap. Kat's heart pounded, her hormones on fire, and her body temperature went up about five hundred degrees. His erection pushed between her thighs, right where she wanted him most. He gripped her ass, and she rocked against him, loving the feel of him through the layers of their clothing.

He held her tight, kissing her forehead, her cheeks, her jaw. Their gazes locked, and she looked deep into him, into the dark pools of his eyes. The happiness that filled her heart was so new, so unexpected, the force of it nearly brought her to tears. She wanted to cling to it, drown in it, and she never, ever, wanted it to end.

"What?" he asked, cupping her face.

She shook her head. There were no words. She closed her eyes and kissed him, saying everything she needed to say with her kiss, hoping that he felt it too. That was impossible, of course, the stuff of fairytales, but she kissed him with everything she had in her, wanting him to know how much he meant to her.

She slipped her hands back inside his shirt and let the downy hair on his chest lead her fingers down. She caressed his stomach, the muscles tightening beneath her fingertips. She racked her fingernails lightly down the rest of his treasure trial. He shuddered when she found him, her hand settling over the bulge in his pants. He was huge, bigger than she could have ever imagined, and she slowly stroked him, taking her time to explore all of him. She wanted to touch him everywhere, taste him, make him moan and shudder. She wanted to lick him, suck him deep, watch the pleasure build on his face.

He gasped and gripped her hand, halting her explorations. His breathing was ragged as he nuzzled her hair and pressed a kiss to her temple. She wrapped her arms around his neck and let him take the lead for now. There was no need to rush. She would have her taste later.

Shivers erupted down her spine when his hand ghosted up her thigh, along the edge of her garter. The look from when they first kissed was there again in his eyes. It was passion and lust, but it was also something so much more.

He held her gaze as he moved his hand higher, his fingers toying with the edge of her panties. She trembled when he traced over her entrance, the thin material hardly any barrier to his caress. Her body screamed for his touch, she arched her back and relaxed her thighs, inviting him in. He hissed through his teeth when dipped his fingers into her hot folds and found her wet and ready.

"I'm going to make love to you *all night*," he whispered, and slid two fingers inside her.

She burned for him, but everything in her froze. Making love? Oh, no. What the hell was she thinking? This was Dean she was messing around with. Of course he was going to blow everything out of proportion and call it making love. It wouldn't be anything else for him. Those two little words meant things that she could never hope to offer him—not in any real way. She was damaged goods, and his expectations were way too high.

His forehead creased, concern furrowing his brow. She sighed when he withdrew his fingers. "Kat?" he asked, gently cupping her mound. "Did I hurt you?"

"No, you didn't hurt me." She stroked his cheek. Oh God, Dean. She wanted him so badly, but he could break her heart. He was the only person on the planet that could. That was a lot of power to give someone—maybe too much.

"What's wrong?" He smoothed the hair off her face. "You don't want to make love? Is it too soon?"

Every time he said it, dual stabs of pleasure and pain pierced her heart. She wished he would shut up so she could maybe pretend that this was just sex, that it didn't have to mean anything, that she wasn't about to risk losing the best friend she'd ever had. "No,

I want..." She couldn't bring herself to say the words. If she said them out loud then everything would permanently change, and there would be no going back. "I want to be with you tonight."

He gave her an odd look, an almost comical twist of his lips, and she might have laughed were it not for the confusion in his eyes. "Then why do you flinch every time I say it?"

"I do not." She tried for indignant, but it came out petulant instead.

He laughed, but it was more from exasperation rather than any real humor. "You do." He cupped her face and made a point of looking directly into her eyes. "Kat, I want to make love to you."

The happiness that thrummed through her was very, very enticing, but she turned away from him, from all that she saw in his gaze. The worst part about it all was that this was what she thought she wanted. Someone to hold. Someone to hold her. He could easily be that man. A part of her desperately wanted that, but the ultimate price was too high. "Come on, Dean, let's just have some fun."

He touched her chin, turning her face back toward him. "This is more than just some fun."

And that was the problem. He was not going to let this be a one-night thing. He was going to want more. He was going to want everything. "Look, this doesn't have to be a big deal, okay?" Emotions rioted through her entire system. It was a big deal, maybe the biggest deal she had ever faced, and she was scared. More than scared, she was flat-out, no joke, petrified. "Nothing has to change," she said, and she heard the plea in her own voice.

He blinked and shook his head, his eyebrows knitted together. "Everything changed when we kissed." He ran his knuckles over her jaw. "You felt it too."

He felt it too! She wanted to weep with joy. And then reality crashed back down. For the most part, Dean was normal. He wanted normal things like family and home and love. She was not normal. There was no way she could ever give him everything he wanted, and consequently, she was going to end up as just another one of his ex-girlfriends. She was not going to let that happen. He was too important to lose. She drew away from him. "I think that it's late. You're tired, you broke up with your girlfriend, it's been—"

"No, no, no," he growled. "Don't do this. I know what you're trying to do and don't do it. This is real."

Every cell in her body screamed for him, but she steeled herself, locking away the dangerous, useless emotions. Sometimes it was so much easier not to feel. "No, it isn't."

He gripped her shoulders, his gaze drilling into hers. "Look at me and tell me this means nothing to you, that you can sleep with me and not feel a thing."

Kat took a deep breath, straightened her spine. Better to end it before it could even begin. It would hurt, but this pain would be nothing compared to the harm they could do to one another if she let this happen. "I can."

He shook his head, never breaking eye contact. "You're lying."

She cut her gaze away. The hurt in his eyes was killing her inside. And because she did love him, more than she had ever loved anyone else, she remained silent.

He let out a disgusted snort, gripped her around the waist and moved her off his lap. When he jumped off the couch, she wanted to reach out to him, draw him back to her side, but she held herself in check. If she allowed herself even one instant of weakness everything would be lost.

He stood over her, his hands on his hips. "So that's it? We have sex and then go back to work and pretend there's nothing more between us. That's what you want?"

That actually sounded pretty good to her. Safe. There was nothing to lose if there was nothing at stake. "That's all there is."

"You're wrong. There's so much more."

Yes, there was. There was so much he didn't know. He led a sheltered life. He didn't know the real power of love, how deeply it could wound. Kat knew. It was a lesson carved into her soul, drilled into her over and over until the day she ran away from home to attend the Art Institute of Chicago. The minute she left her mother's house her life became entirely her own, and she swore that she would never let anybody get close enough to hurt her again. Ever. It was a promise she intended to keep. Dean could devastate her. Even worse, she could seriously damage him too.

She drew into herself, like she had taught herself to do ages ago, and made her heart hard, her insides cold. She met his gaze, resolve freezing the blood in her veins. "Not for us." Her words were tinged with ice and that was just fine. "You should go."

He blinked, looking as though she had slapped him in the face. She supposed in a way she had. He waited for her to say something, anything, but there was nothing more to say. Anger crossed his features, a rage even beyond what she had briefly witnessed during Marine's surprise visit. He gave her one last look, a look of such anger and hurt and love that she nearly gave in. But she couldn't. She just could not. He opened his mouth to say something and then stopped himself with a shake of his head. He turned on his heel, yanked his coat off the rack, and left the apartment. The door closed behind him with a deafening click.

Chapter Four

Dean stormed out of Kat's apartment, turned the corner, and strode up Flatbush Avenue. He needed to put some distance between them, get away from her and the violent, confusing emotions that churned bile in his gut. She was so damn cold, the ice in her gaze an impenetrable glacier. Nothing he said was going to melt that iceberg. Leaving was the best option. Still, it rankled. If only he could shake her out of it, scream at her, do something to break through that frigid veneer. He pressed the heel of his hand over his heart, trying to soothe his thundering pulse. He needed to get a grip. That ice was nothing new. He'd seen it before, witnessed her dismiss all kinds of people from her life without a single flinch. But he never, not in a million-billion years, imagined that she could be that way with him. That's what hurt the most.

The wind sliced through his coat and he pulled it tighter around himself as he entered Prospect Park. He needed to move, to vent some of the needling rage. It was about a half an hour walk back to his place through the park, which wasn't nearly long enough to sufficiently calm him down, but it was going to have to do. Pathetic as he was, he could walk all the way to Jersey if he wanted to and it wouldn't be enough to dispel his pain.

He racked his fingers through his hair, frustration making his blood boil. He must be stupid. He should have done it. He should have fucked her like she wanted, forgot about it on Monday, and gone on with his life. Despite everything, he was still rock-hard for her. Craving her. Her scent was on his skin, her taste in his mouth. There was nothing on this earth like the way she gasped in his ear, her soft pants and whimpers when he touched her, her plump, sexy lips parted, her eyes glazed. He wanted to make her moan, make her writhe and scream and twitch, and he wanted to watch every moment of her pleasure, be right there with her when she gave herself over entirely. He'd never slept with anyone that he hadn't had some kind of feelings for, but maybe she was right, maybe feelings weren't all that important. Maybe they didn't have to be part of the total package. Maybe they just got in the way of the goal.

Dean snorted, his breath a white plume in the night. He could talk all he wanted, but he could never do it. Not with her. Kat may be able to pretend that she could sleep with him and let it go, but he could never be with her halfway, not even in his own imagination.

He licked his bottom lip, savoring the flavor of her there. That first kiss had completely blown him away. He'd never kissed anyone like that before. It was like the kiss from the movies he loved as a child, the ones where the hero saves the world and in the end he gets the girl and the kiss. That one magical kiss meant to last a lifetime. Sappy, but true. And he knew, no matter what she said, she felt it too.

The path wound through the trees, gas lamps lighting the way. He looked up at the moon and sighed as the clouds rolled in, taking over the sky. It was going to snow very soon. He'd better hurry if he wanted to make it home before it started. All this torment and angst was slowing him down. He needed to concentrate. One foot in front of the other. Walk, walk, walk.

He needed to accept that she might be right, that there might not be anything more for them. He was hardly the poster boy for healthy relationships. Why begin something that was only destined to fail? If it ended like any of his others, there would come a time when he would no longer look forward to seeing her in the mornings, to sharing that first cup of coffee of the work day. It wasn't worth losing all that for a few months of happiness.

He arrived at a fork in the path, a crossroads that would either lead him home or circle him back around the park to Kat's neighborhood. He and Kat had gotten sidetracked on this exact path about a year ago. She had sworn that the right-hand path would lead them directly to his apartment, while he was certain that the left was the correct way to go. They couldn't agree, so they decided to walk straight up the middle through the trees and watch for signs on either side to see who was right. Unfortunately, they didn't realize how elaborate the expanse of trees and meadows were between the paths.

Kat would never admit it out loud, but she was a total city girl and deathly afraid of anything she deemed "the woods." He smiled, remembering the way she reached for him when the darkness set in, how she held onto his hand as they stumbled through the trees. They weren't really lost, they were in the middle of Brooklyn, not some remote forest, but she whispered stories of ghosts and goblins to him nonetheless, freaking herself out with her own overactive imagination. He did his best to reassure her that aside from menacing otherworldly creatures, they were quite safe. Her whoop of triumph made him laugh out loud when they exited the greenery, and he'd never forget the way she'd thrown her arms around him, spinning him in circles as she hugged him tight.

The first flakes of snow began to fall and he shivered, more alone than he'd ever been in his life. This was not the way it should be.

A happy couple swept by him, holding hands as they raced off toward their destination. Their laughter filled the otherwise quiet park, whisked from their lips by the burgeoning wind. They took the right-hand path, and his heart ached as he watched them disappear into the night.

Could he have something like that with Kat? Could he really?

Everything in him screamed *Yes!* but a more rational part of his mind actually considered the question. He knew Kat well. Regardless of whatever confidence she exuded, a lot of what drove her was insecurity. She never talked about her childhood—not if she could help it—and the little bit of information he did manage to finagle out of her left him with visions of flying to California to murder her entire family.

She was close-mouthed about everything—her past, her feelings, what she wanted for lunch sometimes. Whenever he got close, she always gently, but firmly, pushed him away. It wasn't just him. She kept the entire world at arm's distance. She was there, but not really involved, alone and fiercely independent.

The wind ruffled his clothes, stirring her scent around him. She wanted him to let her go, but the thought of never laughing with her again, never getting to hold her again, hurt more than anything else on this terrible, awful night. There was no way he wanted to live without her, but he couldn't go back to the way things were. It would be torture to be beside her, yet be unable to touch her. He could not live like that, not with everything that happened tonight. If she was even remotely serious about that blind date, then she was looking for something more. Something real. And it should be with him. She wanted it too. He knew that she did. All the proof was in that kiss. No one kissed like that and didn't mean it.

If this was going to work, then he needed to change up some of his tired, old patterns. Kat was not going to stand for idealized notions or romantic clichés. She was going to force him to face life's inevitable difficulties with her, and not just let him send flowers and hope for the best. Jewelry was not going to impress her. If he wanted her, really wanted her, then he needed to be beside her every step of the way.

And that was only half the battle. It wasn't like she was going to fall into his arms and declare her love. She was going to protest every time he did something for her, complain when he treated her to things, try to push him away at every opportunity. Dean laughed in spite of his misery. It was going to drive her completely insane. He was going to love every minute of it.

"'Let's get ready to rumble,'" he said and smiled. What a night. He took a deep breath and started on the path back to Kat.

* * * * *

Kat stood very still in her living room. She listened to the sound of Dean going down the stairs, heard the front door shut behind him. She could envision him walking down the brownstone's steps, opening the wrought-iron gate, taking a quick right, stopping at corner of Flatbush. She could see him hailing a cab, climbing inside, heading back to Park Slope. Everything was crystal clear in her mind's eye.

She took a deep breath, let it out. The silence in her apartment was massive, like standing in a gigantic bubble. She supposed she should maybe sit down, have a drink, get undressed or do something besides standing frozen in place in the middle of the room. But there really didn't seem to be any point, and a small part of her worried that if she moved, even a fraction of an inch, that bubble would burst and maybe she would discover that she wasn't quite as cold as she thought she was. And that would be unacceptable.

Her gaze drifted toward the triple-bay windows and the monstrous sculpture that sat between them in all its ugly steel and pink spray-paint glory. She loved that statue, was taken with it the first time she saw it in the gallery window, the way it drew her out of the line of commuters trudging their way down Spring Street, made her stop and stare. Every day on her way to and from work she stopped to look at it, captivated by its dementedness. On one of the rare occasions Dean took the subway instead of biking into the city, he noticed her attraction. When he asked her about it, she dismissed it as a useless trinket, something destined only to collect dust. It was that for sure, but it was also strangely appealing in its own worthless way. She had been crushed the day it was no longer on display. Then, two days later, it arrived at her door with a note that read: *Things that bring you joy are never useless. Happy merry unbirthday! Love, Dean.*

Prickly heat torched her cheeks and she fought against the sensations that threatened to penetrate her void. She turned away from the statue, needing to concentrate on anything else, and a flash of bright yellow caught her eye, drawing her attention to the coat rack. The hideous ski coat Dean kept forgetting to take home rested there, clashing with all her dark coats, an obnoxious splash of lunatic brightness in a sea of black.

Kat grimaced. That damn coat. That was the night that started everything, that set this whole terrible chain of events in motion.

It was the day after Thanksgiving, and Kat was sitting on her couch touching up a trilogy of comics she intended to post over Christmas. She hadn't left her apartment since she arrived there on Wednesday afternoon, hadn't talked to anyone or answered her phone. She worked in total silence, never noticing the passing of the hours until she looked up and found it dark. Yesterday, she was so wrapped up in her work, she had almost forgotten to eat her store-bought turkey dinner.

She was finishing off some background shading when the doorbell rang, nearly making her jump out of her skin. The sound of her pounding heart was as loud as the snap of the deadbolt coming unlocked. Only one person had the key to her place, yet she was shocked right down to her newly painted toenails when Dean walked through the door.

"What are you doing here?" she asked, looking at him over her laptop. He caught her completely offguard, and she was more than a little embarrassed to be seen in her boxer shorts and old tank top, no makeup, and messy house hair.

He grinned like the madman he was. He was wearing a massive yellow ski coat even though the week had been unseasonably warm. With his dark pants and heavy boots, it was like he had come in from the arctic rather than a pleasant, sunny afternoon. He closed the door behind himself and held up a brown takeout bag. "Happy Thanksgiving!"

She laughed. How could she not? He was insane. She put her laptop aside and crossed the room to greet him. She stood on her tip-toes to kiss him hello, very aware of how thin her shirt was. Maybe if she ignored the fact that she wasn't wearing a bra, he wouldn't notice. He wound his arm around her waist and she was enveloped in his warmth, the scent of his cologne. Dean gave the best hugs.

She hugged him back and then took a step away from him. "Seriously, Dean, what are you doing here? I thought you were going to see your family?"

"I did. I just came back a little early." He held up the bag. "I tried to call you yesterday, but you didn't answer. It's bad luck to spend Thanksgiving alone."

"Is it?" She was achingly touched. He came back to New York for her. "I never heard that before." She fingered the lift tickets hanging from the zipper on his jacket. "Did you come straight from the airport?"

"Pretty much. It's warm here." He put the bag aside and stripped off his coat and sweater, tossed them on the coat rack.

She needed to do something, distract herself from the crazy emotions that wanted to choke her. She reached for food, but he was too quick, snatching up again before she could get it. "What have you got there?" she asked.

"Brazilian takeout."

Kat snorted. "How very traditional."

"Well, I know you have a weakness for *brigadeiro*." He gave her a sheepish grin. "And it was the only thing open."

She lunged for the bag again, but he held it out of reach. "Okay, fine. If you won't give it up, then go grab some plates." She waved toward the kitchen. "I have to put some clothes on."

His gaze was like a physical caress and her cheeks flushed, but not from embarrassment. "You look great," he said softly.

She was pleased by the compliment, but he was always full of nice words for the ladies, so she decided not to acknowledge it. "I'll meet you in kitchen."

They feasted while drinking red wine and talking of minor things. She wasn't really one for the holiday spirit or anything, but that night she saw the appeal. And she was truly thankful.

When he left, taking his sweater but not his coat, her apartment seemed lifeless and bland. The sudden quiet took on a different meaning, and instead of being a comfort, it was now an absence, a silent, sucking void. For the first time ever, she realized how lonely she truly was. And how much she didn't like it.

When Ron offered her the date, she'd hoped to find a way to fill that void, to calm the restlessness. She thought all she wanted was to feel that hot spark of tension with someone and still be about to talk with them about pointless things.

But what she really wanted was Dean.

A shiver ran over her and her resolve crumbed, the bubble shattered. She crashed down on the couch with a strangled groan, clenching her fists to stem the torrent of emotion. Her chest ached, tears threatened, but she held herself tightly in check. She would get on top of this, dammit. She did not need him. This was not a big deal. She had survived just fine for years and years before she met him. She would survive many more without him.

Out of habit, she pressed her fingers to her mouth, but the touch recharged her sensitive lips, recalling the thrill of his kiss. That awesome kiss. The way he licked her tongue sent chills right down to her tippy-toes. She smiled. He was a great kisser. The taste of him lingered in her memory, the heat of him in her hand, the vibrations of his moans. Arousal sizzled through her bloodstream. There were still so many ways she'd like to make him moan.

A car backfired and Kat came back to herself with a start. "Stupid," she said aloud, shaking her head. What the hell was she doing? Thoughts like that were only going to make her insane.

Her gaze touched on his coat again and her heart cried out for him. She groaned. Dean always made everything so fucking difficult. Even before the kiss, he had always gotten under her skin. He was her one exception, the asterisk on her every rule. She was never going to have any peace if she didn't find some way to reconcile with him.

Kat hugged herself tightly. Something different. That was what she thought she wanted. Well, kissing Dean had certainly been different. And wonderful. But the feelings were too real, too... *much*. She needed something safer, something risk-free. She obviously couldn't handle anything more complex. The first chance she got, she reverted back to her default state of breezy, free-and-easy sex. Eric would have been perfect. They had no history and nothing to lose—a clean slate.

Dean was in a whole other league. If it didn't work out with him—if she failed—she would have to forfeit the very best part of her life. There would be no more late-night talks, no more creative endeavors, no more troublesome fun. Everything would be lost. He had to realize that. Maybe if she explained it better, outlined all the risks calmly and logically, he would understand.

She jumped to her feet. That was it! She just needed to explain to him how disastrous it would be for them to hook up and then everything would be fine. Just like always. This was too important to wait until Monday. A phone call would not work. She had to see him. Now. Before things got any worse. She grabbed her keys and her phone and snatched the first coat she touched off the rack, which happened to be Dean's yellow eyesore. The scent of his cologne enveloped her as she exited the apartment, running down the stairs as fast as her heels and party dress would allow. Puffy snowflakes rained from the sky, and a hush fell over the city as a fine layer of snow coated the sidewalks. She raced to Flatbush, searching for a cab. The dollar van came rambling up the avenue and she flagged it down. It reeked of wet carpet, and she sat on the edge of the worn cloth seat, trying to work out everything she needed to say to him.

The van deposited her about a block from his place. When she got to his building, she jogged up the stairs and into the foyer. She let herself in with her key and went directly to his apartment. She knocked once and then entered, only to find it dark and deserted.

"Dammit!" she spat out and stomped her foot. A childish move, but she couldn't help herself.

Her phone vibrated and she hastily fished it out of the coat's voluminous pocket. Dean's ridiculous selfie illuminated the screen. Her heart exploded to life, nerves, joy, desire making her hands shake. She slid the accept call bar across the screen. "Where are you?" she asked, too overwrought to bother with the pleasantries.

"I'm at your place." She couldn't quite believe how good it was to hear his voice, the way the sound of filled her up inside. "Where are you?"

Kat closed her eyes as anxiety, relief, and pure, unabashed love for him washed over her. He had gone back for her. She should have known. "I'm at your place."

He let out a huff that was almost a laugh. "Stay where you are. I'll be there soon."

"Okay," she said, not wanting to argue. All she wanted was to see him again—the sooner the better.

She ended the call, took off his coat, tossed it aside. There was nothing to do now but wait. With the snow coming, it was probably going to take him a while to get home. She flipped on the light. Nervous energy propelled her around the room. It was going to be fine when she saw him. This was Dean. She didn't have anything to be afraid of. They would work it out. They had to. The alternative was unthinkable.

She touched the mantel over his fireplace as she paced, the back of the sofa, the bookshelves. The plug-in air freshener puffed out a hint of warm amber. His living room was a familiar place, comfortable, and filled with happiness. She sat down on his plush easy chair—her chair—the spot where she had spent many a night hatching crazy schemes and partaking in drunken antics, indulging in long, intense talks, philosophical debates and mad laughter.

Her gaze touched on the colorful arrangement of framed photographs hanging on the wall behind the sofa and she smiled. There was Dean young and old, with his parents, his brother, graduating from college, completing his first marathon. And she was there as well, there beside him, their arms thrown up to the heavens as they screamed their way down the steepest plunge on the Cyclone, and there again with his arm around her waist, her hand on his knee, laughing uproariously together at the company picnic.

The memories flowed over her and she closed her eyes against the rising tide of emotion that wanted to carry her away. She loved him so much. It would be so much easier if she didn't.

The door opened and Kat's breath caught. She rose to her feet and met his eyes. Her resolution almost wavered. Almost. "It would never work between us," she blurted out, all the carefully chosen words she had prepared on the way over flying right out of her head.

He just raised an eyebrow and closed the door behind himself.

"Think about it, Dean. I'm so not your type," she went on as he shook the snow out of his hair and hung his coat up in the closet by the door. "You need a woman who wants to rely on you, someone you can care for, and you know that's not me. You know how crazy it makes me when you do it, imagine having to deal with that every day. All my bitching would get old very quickly." She was babbling and she knew it, but she didn't care. He needed to *understand*. She had to make this right.

He didn't say anything, simply strode across the living room and entered the kitchen. She followed behind him and watched as he opened one of the top cabinets, pulled out a bottle of Jack. He held it up to her and she nodded in reply.

"I really don't have the time for a relationship anyway," she said as he got glasses out of another cabinet and poured two healthy shots. "You know how much my work means to me." She accepted the glass from him and downed the whiskey. "I need to give it all of my attention."

He took his shot, placed his glass on the kitchen table, and then marched toward her. He towered over her, crowding her, backing her up against the wall. His palms slapped down on either side of her head and she was trapped, caged beneath his body. And then, his lips were on hers. It was the most natural thing in the world to open for him, so she did, letting him slip his tongue deep into her mouth.

Hunger exploded in her core, a violent wave of red-hot desire, and she wrapped her arms around his neck. That special, wonderful feeling that only he inspired rushed through her veins. It was everything she had ever been missing in her life, everything she had always secretly hoped for, but was afraid of needing. Connection. Warmth. Affection. She leaned into him and their hips met, pressed together. He pulled her into his arms and flames ignited in her lower belly, a rush of heat and desire and something more powerful than lust.

He pulled back suddenly, leaving her panting, breathless. His eyes flashed in the dim light. "Tell me you don't feel that."

She slumped back against the wall, all the fight drained out of her. "Of course I do."

He gripped her upper arms, frustration and relief warring on his handsome face. "Then I don't understand what the problem is."

She threw up her hands, knocking him aside. "You're the problem." She crossed the room to put some space between them. It was hard to think with him so close, especially since all she really wanted to do was kiss him again. She turned her back to him and stared out his kitchen window, watching the snow fall. "This is going to end badly and…" She let out a shaky breath, trying to calm the tumult of emotions within her. "And I don't want to lose you," she said, unable to keep the desperation out of her voice.

"What makes you think you're going to lose me?"

Kat rolled her eyes and looked at him over her shoulder.

She should not have been surprised to see that he was honestly perplexed. "Everything ends, Dean."

He held her gaze. "That's not true."

"Oh, no? How long have your relationships ever lasted?" There was that venom she loved to employ. Lashing out was one of the many horrendous things she was good at. And it was another reason why being with him was such a bad idea. She didn't want to hurt him—not ever—and yet here she was, doing it like a champ.

"We can make it work."

She scoffed, shook her head.

"Look, I know you think it's all bullshit, but people need love. It's important. I've made plenty of mistakes. I know what a crappy boyfriend I can be, but I think with you around to keep me honest, I can learn to be better." He took a single step toward her. "It's going to suck sometimes, that's for sure, and yeah, we'll probably fight. But we'll make up too. And we'll laugh. And we'll wake up together." He placed his hands on the island between them and leaned forward. "You and I—we're different. This isn't anything like Marine or any of the others. I think you know that. What we have is real, Kat. I'm not going to let you just walk away."

She wanted to believe him, but she could not afford to get caught up in his romantic delusions. She turned back to the window, watching the world outside turn white. A chilly draft touched her skin as the wind rattled the glass, and she folded her arms over her breasts. Alone. This was the way she needed to be. She was safe this way.

She heard him behind her, listened as he crossed the room, and felt the weight of his presence by her side. He touched her hair and then rested his hands on her shoulders. "Do you trust me?"

He was the one person she did trust. The only one. That damn lump formed in her throat again, and she swallowed hard to try to get rid of it. "I don't trust myself."

He wrapped his arms around her, holding her close. She wanted to resist, but it felt so good to be held, to be enveloped in his warmth. "I trust you," he whispered in her ear.

Her resolve was slipping away, but she couldn't give in. "You also thought mauve was the perfect color for that death metal band's website."

He squeezed her tighter. "Kat…"

She had to make a decision. What she said next was going to change everything between them forever. Here was her chance for something new. Was she brave enough to take the dream being offered? There was only one way to find out. "I'll try."

He pressed his cheek against hers. "'Do or do not. There is no try.'"

Kat groaned, trying to smother the laughter that wanted to tumble out of her. How did he always manage to do that to her? "I can't believe you're quoting *Star Wars* to me right now."

"It was either that or *The Little Engine That Could*. I felt that Yoda was the better choice." She heard the smile in his voice.

"Okay," she said, finally giving in. A lead cloud of terror began to gather in her chest, but she forced it back. She made her decision. It was time to live with it. "Let's go."

He kissed her cheek and gently rocked her in his arms as they stood quietly together in front of the window watching the snow blanket the street.

"It's pretty bad out there," he said, resting his chin on her shoulder.

She nodded. It was coming down hard. "I wonder if I'll be able to find a cab home."

He moved behind her, a subtle shift of his hips that made everything go liquid inside her. "Stay."

Kat's cheeks flushed as heat flared in her veins. This new dimension of their relationship had definite perks. She turned around to face him and curled her arms around his neck. The desire in his eyes sent a very satisfying wave of lust straight to her deepest core. She could get very used to this. "Hmm, I don't know. I think you might have nefarious intentions in mind."

"Nefarious intentions?" he asked, grinning broadly. He pretended to think it over as his hands moved over the curve of her waist to grip her ass. "Yes, that sounds right."

She had to bite her lower lip to hold back her squeal of laughter when he groped her. "Good," she said, rubbing against him. Rigid heat pressed against her hip. "Those are my favorite kind of intentions."

He maneuvered her backward, using teasing kisses and nips to guide her where he wanted her. Her ass hit the window sill, and he lifted her onto the ledge. She pressed her chest against his, felt his heart beat along with her own. Her fingers tangled in his hair, the kiss went longer, deeper, his tongue thrusting in and out of her mouth, making her go slick with anticipation. He licked her bottom lip and pulled back, grinning as he looked down into her eyes. "You should probably know that I also have wanton and depraved intentions in mind."

She smiled. Sleeping with him was going to be incredible. His shirt was still halfway unbuttoned and she slipped her hands inside it, caressing his chest. "That's quite an agenda," she said, and flicked his nipple.

A shudder rolled over him as she teased the hard nub. He took her hand, brought it to his mouth and bit down lightly on her knuckle. "You are such a bad girl." He licked the pads of her fingers and then placed her hand over the bulge in his jeans. "What am I going to do with you?"

She gave him a little squeeze. "What do you want to do with me?"

He grinned and nudged her thighs apart. When he captured her mouth again, she wrapped her leg around his waist. His hips moved and she gasped, her head falling back against the window as molten heat flooded her panties. He thrust again and she moaned, spreading her legs wider for him.

"Look at me," he said, and she lifted her head to meet his eyes. "I want to make love to you, Kat."

Her heart hammered an exhilarating tempo. "Yes."

He looked deep into her. "This is not just sex."

The truth washed over, nerves and elation making her blood pressure spike. "No."

"Say it," he commanded. "Tell me what this is."

She caressed his cheek. "You say those words so easily. It's not that easy for me."

He looked into her eyes, steadfast, beautiful Dean, earnest as ever and twice as sincere. "It is that easy."

She shook her head. "I didn't grow up in the most nurturing environment. My mother and I…well, we have a lot of issues."

He tucked a strand of her hair behind her ear. "I kind of figured."

"Yeah, it can be rough." She stared at the linoleum floor. How could she make him understand? "The first time I realized how awful love could be, I was five years old." She'd never told anyone what she was about to tell him. It was her darkest secret and deepest shame. "My mother and I were living with my grandfather at the time. My mom was out of work and my dad…" She paused. There was no way to sugar-coat any of it. "My dad was wanted by the police for some reason or another, probably fraud. It was his favorite thing. My grandfather hated my father and my mother would sneak out to visit him in secret."

Her distress was clearly bothering him. She'd never seen him look so worried. "Kat, you don't have to do this."

"No, I do. You should understand. And I need to tell you. So, just listen, okay?"

He nodded once. "Okay."

She took a deep breath before she continued. "One day, I was allowed to go along with her. I don't know why. That had never happened before. I was always left home alone to my own devices when my mother went to meet him. I didn't mind. I liked it that way. I rarely got to go out all, and it was the thought of getting into the car more than seeing my father that really thrilled me." She smiled, but there was no humor, only unrelenting sadness. "Because there was this toy, this Happy Meal toy, that I wanted more than anything in the world. And if we were going out, it meant we could get it. It was *limited edition*, you see, and the TV kept telling me I had to *act now*. If I didn't get it soon, it would be lost forever. I wanted it so badly. I begged her to stop at McDonald's."

She licked her dry lips, and Dean drew her closer. "My mother was in no mood to argue. She wanted to see my dad, be with him for at least a little while. She agreed to stop because she knew it was the quickest way to shut me up. Before we left, she called my dad to rearrange the meeting location." She pressed her lips together. "Neither of us realized my grandfather was listening. When we got to McDonald's, the police were waiting."

Inhale, she told herself. Exhale. Breathe. "We walked through the glass doors, and my father fought back when two plainclothes detectives tackled him. There was blood." She swallowed hard, reliving the moment, once again assaulted by the shame, the terror, the confusion. "I was scared. I was five. I didn't know what was going on. Strange men were hurting my dad." She looked up at the ceiling, trying to blink back the tears that wanted to form. "All I wanted was my mommy."

She barely noticed when he shifted his weight and resettled his arms around her waist. She was lost in the past. "I reached out to take her hand, but she snarled, pulled away. 'Look at what you caused,' she said, stabbing the air in front of my face with her long, red fingernail. 'You just got your father arrested. Are you happy?'"

She remembered it all so clearly, every detail of the formica tables, the bright-yellow walls, the smell of French fries and hot apples pies, the other children crying from the commotion. "I saw in her eyes how much she hated me. I didn't understand what that actually meant until much later, though. All I knew then was that I had done something terribly wrong and I deserved to cry alone."

"Kat," he said, breaking into her dreadful reverie. "None of that has anything to do with love."

She sighed. "But it does. Don't you see? The only reason any of it mattered was because I loved her. I thought if I could be cold, if I could not care, then she couldn't hurt me. I tried so hard, but I couldn't do it. Not enough, anyway."

She looked away from him, but he caught her chin and lifted her face up to meet his gaze. "I love you."

Her mouth fell open. "Are you fucking insane? I tell you the most traumatic experience of my childhood, the very reason why I don't trust in love, and you tell me you love me?"

"Yeah," he said, grinning like a lunatic. "I love you. I want you to know that because I want you to know what love really means. It has nothing to with any part of what you told me." He gathered her closer. "Love is a good thing, Kat. It's not a weapon or a punishment."

She could only shake her head. "You're crazy."

"Crazy in love."

She didn't want to laugh, but she did. She didn't want to feel the big, fat, sloppy explosion of emotions in her heart either, but she felt those too. "You have no idea what you're getting yourself into."

He smiled. "I think I do."

Maybe he did. He did seem to know her far better than she liked to admit sometimes. "What if I can't say it?"

He cupped her face in his hands. "You can."

And for him, she did. "I love you, Dean."

He kissed her nose. "See? That wasn't so hard, was it?"

No, it wasn't. In fact, it felt rather good, much better than she would have ever expected. "So, what, we live happily ever after now?"

"Eventually. But we have something else to do first." His hands moved to her waist, his thumbs resting just below her breasts.

"We do?" she asked, drawing him closer.

"Yes. There's something I've been wanting to know for a while now." He kissed her throat, nuzzled her ear. "Something I'm very curious about."

"Hmmm," she said, her insides melting as he nibbled her

shoulder. "What's that?"

He cupped her face in his hands. "I want to know what you look like when you come."

Scorching chills raced over as skin. "Well, there's something I've been curious about too."

"Really?" he asked, slowly tracing the line of her cleavage. "Do tell."

She kissed his lips, his cheek, his jaw. "I want to know what your cock tastes like," she whispered in his ear.

He licked her neck, fondling her breast. "It tastes pretty good. I think you're going to like it."

She did her best to hold back her laughter, but a few chuckles spilled out. She reached between them and gently cupped him. "You do have a lot to offer."

He ran his index finger over her bottom lip. "It's all for you." He met her gaze. "Only you."

She never thought she'd be such sucker for sentimentality, but he did the strangest things to her heart and her head. Wonderful things. She touched her lips to his for a soft kiss. "You're damn right it is."

She screamed laughter when he scooped her up, tossed her over his shoulder, and carried her off to his bedroom. He dumped her on his bed and bent to kiss her, but she pushed him away with a playful grin.

"You know," she said, running her fingers over the swell of her breasts. His eyes followed the path of her hand and she had to admit she very much enjoyed his rapt attention. "I always thought of 'making love' as something prim, kind of stodgy." She hooked her finger under one of the straps on her dress and slowly dragged it down her shoulder. "Like strictly missionary."

He knelt down before her, his face level with her breasts. "Missionary is nice," he said, reaching around her to unzip her dress. "But any way I'm inside you is going to be making love." He slid the dress down and off her body. "The position doesn't matter."

She unbuttoned the remaining buttons on his shirt, stripping it off him. "So, let's say I want you cowgirl style." She scraped her fingers lightly down his chest, gripped his belt buckle. "When I'm riding you as hard as I can, is that still going to be making love?"

"Yes," he said, his hands moving up her legs, his fingertips skimming over her thighs. "And when I've got you on all-fours." A few flicks of his wrist and her garters came undone. "And I'm taking you from behind." Her bra went next. "And your legs are shaking because you need to come so bad." He gripped her panties and yanked them down. "And you scream out my name because I feel so fucking good in you." He crawled on the bed beside her and cupped her mound. "That's going to be making love too."

"Oh, Dean," she whimpered when slid two fingers inside her. She panted out inarticulate moans as he stroked her, her hips catching his rhythm. The building tension made her quake, and she gripped his wrist, her nails digging into his flesh. He curled his fingers and brilliant light exploded behind her eyelids.

"Let me see you come, Kat." His thumb circled her clit and his fingers pressed deeper.

Her back arched off the bed as the orgasm took her, wracking her body with violent waves of pleasure. He murmured in her ear as she writhed, soft spoken words of love and encouragement. The ecstasy went on and on, his clever fingers teasing every drop of her. He didn't stop until she screamed, helpless cries of mindless bliss. Electric currents shot through veins even as she came down, and he brushed the damp hair off her face as she caught her breath, gently soothing her as her heart rate returned to more normal zones.

"That was the most beautiful thing I have ever seen," he said, and reverence in his voice only made her love him more.

She reached for him, needing him like wildfire, still throbbing and far from sated. She gripped his belt, her fingers fumbling on the buckle. The button his jeans wouldn't unhook and the zipper caught as she tried to yank it down. She tugged frantically, finally getting it to release and pushed his pants down. His cock rested against his belly, hot and thick and hard. He shuddered when she gripped him, and his Adam's apple bobbed in his throat when she stroked the full length of him. "I want you." She gave him a little tug. "Now."

He kissed her hard, got off the bed, and went to the bedside table. The drawer squeaked as it slid open. He rummaged around, found a roll of condoms, tore one off the strip and held it in his teeth as he pushed his jeans the rest of the way off. He was so beautiful in the low light of the room, his body a chiseled work of art, hard muscle sculpted from years of working out and sports. She still couldn't quite believe that he was hers. Her heart beat a little faster, and the smile that settled on her lips warmed her whole body.

He rolled the condom on and she opened her arms to him, welcoming his weight as he settled on top of her. His head nudged her outer folds and she looked up at him and smiled wider. She arched her hips and he guided himself slowly inside.

She gasped when he thrust all the way in and they both froze, locked into one another. Time stretched out, an infinity of pleasure captured in a single, endless moment. Their breathing synced as they held one another, joined for the first time.

"Oh, God, Kat," he rasped and touched his forehead to hers.

A sobbing moan wracked her body when he slid out and then all the way back in again. She gripped his ass, biting into his shoulder as the slow, deep, controlled thrust rocked her world. Every plunge heightened her need and her body demanded more, wanting him harder, faster. She brought her hips up hard against his, quickening their pace. He came up on his knees, forcing her legs up onto his shoulders, spreading her thighs wide apart. She raked her nails up his back, groaning out exquisite pleasure when he plunged deeper into her, filling her completely. It was total sensory overload, and in that instant she finally understood why "making love" was so different and special. He was physically in her body and forged in her heart as well.

He touched his tongue to hers and they moaned together as their bodies joined and parted and joined again. He thrust harder, his hips grinding against hers and she met him again and again. Panting, kissing, licking, biting, they brought each other higher, until the tension was so sweet it was nearly unbearable. Her fingers dug into his ass as rapture seized her again, her eyes squeezing shut as the euphoria took her.

"No," he said, cupping her face in both of his hands. "Open your eyes. Look at me."

She obeyed instantly, looking into him as she came, holding his gaze until she was blind from the enormity of her pleasure.

When he found his release, he captured her mouth, not in a tender kiss, but one of pure possession. He plunged into her hard, claiming her now with every thrust. The orgasm shuddered through him, and he emptied himself with a long, low growl.

She collapsed beneath him, spent and satisfied, and the room echoed with the heavy sound of their breathing.

After a moment he stirred, kissing her lips, brushing her damp hair off her forehead. He propped himself up on his elbows and nipped her shoulder. "Tired?"

Kat laughed. "Not yet."

"Good," he said, and this time they took it nice and slow.

* * * * *

Hours later, Dean lay between her thighs, his head resting on her hip, tracing lazy patterns on her lower belly with his index finger. "How many times do you think we're going to hear, 'I told you so'?"

She stroked his hair, a slow, leisurely caress, her fingers gliding through his golden-brown curls. "Hmmm, five hundred and twenty-seven," she guessed. "And that'll just be on Monday."

He chuckled, his breath tickling her tummy.

She floated somewhere between sleep and consciousness, utterly

74

relaxed and completely fulfilled. She drifted in the hazy bliss until a sudden, dreadful thought occurred to her. "Don't think this means I'm going to start jogging with you or anything, you crazy lunatic," she said, and tapped him lightly on the head. "I mean it, Dean. No running or hiking or biking or any of that crap."

"That's all right. I can think of other ways to keep you in shape." His hand glided over her inner thigh and heat instantly ignited in her core. If tonight was any indication of how things were going to be, she was probably going to be able to run marathons with him before too long.

She traced the muscles in his shoulders, the line of his biceps. "There's still time to end this," she said, though the words made her heart ache. "Go back to the way things were."

He shifted his weight, resting his chin on her tummy to look up at her. "Is that what you want?"

That selfish little part of her roared to life, vehemently rejecting the notion of never getting to touch him again. And for once, she decided to listen to it. "No," she said, quietly. "I don't want that at all."

He held her gaze and pressed a kiss to her stomach. "Neither do I."

She closed her eyes and lay back on the pillows. Everything in her was at peace. She gave his scalp a gentle scratch with her fingernails. This must be what happiness is, she decided. It was a feeling she wanted to get very used to.

"You know," Dean said, crawling up her body to lie down beside her. "We're going to have to get married now."

Laughter erupted out of her. "Oh yeah? Why is that?"

"Well, it is part of that happily-ever-after thing." He put his arm around her shoulders and she rested her head on his chest. "And because this is never going to end."

"And marriage is going to guarantee that?" she asked, nuzzling his jaw.

"Of course. Through the power of solemn vows and wearing

white…" He pinched her side and she laughed. "You'll be my beautiful blushing bride. We'll move to the suburbs, have kids—lots and lots of kids—and an SUV and—"

"Stop!" She was horrified, appalled, but also oddly taken with the notion. "You're freaking me out."

He grinned. "I'm just telling you like it is."

"Let's talk about it next year," she said. "I can only take one life-altering change per calendar year."

"All right," he said, running his fingers up and down her spine. "Next year."

Kat rolled her eyes even as she smiled. She knew that tone in his voice all too well. He was not going to let that subject drop. Still, the thought of being with him every day, for forever and ever… well, it wasn't a bad thought at all. Maybe she wouldn't protest too hard when he brought it up again.

He touched her cheek, turning her face to his. "Tell me that you love me."

She almost choked on the raw emotion that filled her throat. Was it always going to be like this with him? God, she hoped so. "I love you, Dean."

He held her gaze and laced his fingers through hers. "We are forever, Kat. Never doubt that."

"Forever," she agreed and squeezed his hand. After tonight, she was willing to believe it could be true.

He kissed her lightly on the lips and gathered her closer. She snuggled deep down into his embrace. The steady rhythm of his heartbeat lulled her to sleep, and she drifted off, warm and safe in his arms.